DEVIL'S
FOOTSTEPS

ALSO BY E. E. RICHARDSON

The Intruders

DEVIL'S
FOOTSTEPS

E. E. Richardson

LAUREL-LEAF BOOKS

Published by Laurel-Leaf
an imprint of Random House Children's Books
a division of Random House, Inc.
New York

Originally published in Great Britain
by Random House UK, London, in 2005.
This edition published by arrangement with Delacorte Press.

www.randomhouse.com/teens
Educators and librarians, for a variety of teaching tools,
visit us at www.randomhouse.com/teachers

RL: 5.9
ISBN-13: 978-0-440-23916-1
ISBN-10: 0-440-23916-8

November 2006
Printed in the United States of America
10 9 8 7 6 5 4 3 2 1
First Laurel-Leaf Edition

DEVIL'S
FOOTSTEPS

One in fire, two in blood

"Come on, Bryan!"

Three in storm and four in flood

"What the hell are you so afraid of?"

Five in anger, six in hate

"You don't seriously believe this junk, do you?"

Seven fear and evil eight

"You think the Dark Man's gonna come and get me?"

Nine in sorrow, ten in pain

"It's just a stupid game."

Eleven death, twelve life again

"It's like a skipping rhyme."

Thirteen steps to the Dark Man's door

"You ever see anybody die from a skipping rhyme, Bryan?"

Won't be turning back no more

Adam!

Bryan woke, as he always did, with a scream that didn't really happen out loud, and the sweat sticking the cotton sheets together. It was the height of summer and school was nearly out, the grass outside was dying, and even in the shade the concrete was hot to the touch. But Bryan was still shivering.

The shivers always came in summer.

People thought winter was the bad time, the time when you huddled under your blankets and hid from the evil things outside. But winter was just dull and dark. It had to be bright and sunny for the blackest shadows to come out.

He could always feel the Dark Man when the weather started to warm up. It was his season. The sun in the sky and the birds in the trees, and the Dark Man in the shadows.

He'd tried to tell himself again and again that it was imagination, twisted memories. He'd only been ten when it happened; he was fifteen now. He had been just a kid, and his brain had made him see the Dark Man because that was what they'd been playing. The Devil's Footsteps were just stones, and the Dark Man hadn't taken Adam.

But it was Adam's voice Bryan heard when he told himself that. Adam laughing, taunting, making fun of Bryan, who hadn't completed the rhyme, who'd run away before he'd reached the thirteenth step. Adam making fun of the Dark Man.

What did it matter if you believed in the legend or not? Adam was still gone.

Everybody laughed if you mentioned the Dark Man. A local myth, the children's bogeyman. The Dark Man of Redford. What a silly, childish story. Everybody laughed. And everybody hugged their coats about them and said, "Hey, isn't it cold in here? I think it's going to be a bad winter, this one."

2

Bryan could have told them that it wasn't winter you had to watch out for. He might be fifteen now, but you don't grow out of childhood superstitions when you've seen them with your own eyes.

But Bryan just wiped the cold sweat away, and got out of bed. Because being afraid of the Dark Man didn't get you a day off school. Not even a missing brother did that, five years down the line.

His parents were already downstairs, making breakfast, talking quietly. It looked happy, it all looked normal. Only if you'd been here five years before could you tell that something had changed, something was missing. Something that should have been here had slipped out into the night and disappeared with Adam. His parents might be making conversation, but Bryan didn't think either of them was really listening to it.

The dining table had four chairs, and no matter where you sat you shared it with the ghost of Adam. Bryan poured himself a bowl of Cheerios and sat on the arm of a chair in the living room to eat them. Adam's face smiled up at him from the photographs. But that was better than the other photographs, the later ones, the ones with the Adam-shaped hole in them.

The smiles all looked the same. Even his own. Bryan always thought that was creepiest of all, that it all looked the same and you couldn't see. That there could be this great big huge *wrongness* in the middle of their family, and you couldn't actually see it at all.

He was always glad to get outside. Even in the summer, when the Dark Man might be out there waiting for him, it was better to be outside. Being at home was like sitting in a crypt where they'd forgotten to tell the people they were dead.

3

As he walked, he counted steps. He always did it, he didn't know how to stop.

One in fire. Two in blood. Three in storm. Four in flood.

Devil's Footsteps was one of those playground rhymes that everybody knew and nobody remembered making up. It was a game, a test of bravery. Whichever step you stopped on, that told you how you would die.

Five in anger. Six in hate. Seven fear. Evil eight.

But somewhere out in the woods, so the legend went, were the *real* Devil's Footsteps. A trail of stones that led nowhere. And if you walked the real Devil's Footsteps and you said the rhyme, then on the thirteenth step the Dark Man would come to claim you.

And he and Adam had found them. He had been ten years old, and he'd believed it. His nerve had broken on the eleventh step, and he'd jumped off the stones and fled back to the beginning. He was too afraid of the Dark Man. Adam had been twelve and he hadn't believed, because twelve-year-olds had no time for stupid games like Devil's Footsteps. But he'd had to prove to Bryan just how childish he was being. He'd had to get all the way to the thirteenth step.

Afterwards, of course, there had been news bulletins and posters pinned to trees, and quiet patient policemen who tried to get him to *describe* this "Dark Man," tell them about the person who'd taken his brother. There had been search parties who methodically quartered the woods, going over every inch, missing nothing.

None of them had ever found thirteen stones that made a pathway. And none of them had ever found Adam.

But life went on. He hadn't believed it could, that long-ago summer, but it had just kept rolling on. September had come around, and school had started again, and there he was, back at school without Adam. And now here he was, Year Eleven, while Adam was still frozen back in time five years ago, twelve years old forever.

But in a way, that helped. Bryan had never shared these corridors with Adam, and there were no ghosts to follow him around. And in the press of students, a mass of kids and teachers greater than anything Bryan had ever imagined back when he was ten, there was no room for the Dark Man. The Dark Man didn't like crowds.

Bryan arrived early, as he always did, and waited alone in the library for the bell. It wasn't that he was particularly lonely or isolated in school; people talked to him, and he talked to them, but he never sought out company. When he was younger, there had always been Adam to be close with, and after his brother had gone he'd just never really tried to fill the gap. He wouldn't have wanted to bring friends back to visit his poisoned home; nor would he want to visit them, look around at their families and sense that thing that was missing from his own.

He didn't know how many of the other kids knew about his family tragedy; five years was a long time, and only a handful of those from his old junior school had followed him to this one. But they seemed to be on some level aware of it, willing to leave him alone when he wanted to be. The teachers were the same, never trying to pull him into the core of the group or trying to make him talk about it. Maybe it was something about the town of Redford; people here never seemed to want to push at things like that, as if they were afraid of uncovering something that was better left buried.

So it was unusual, if not totally unheard of, when Stephen

came into the library right on his heels and sat across from him.

Stephen Bacon—handsome and chocolate-skinned—was a good-natured, talkative boy; neither a brain nor a trouble-maker, and certainly not the kind of social outcast who would need to seek out someone like Bryan Holden for company.

"Bryan, can I talk to you a minute?" There was an oddly hesitant note to his voice.

Bryan blinked, and pushed aside his book. "Sure, Stephen, what's up?" He and Stephen shared a few classes, but they rarely exchanged more than a "hi."

"I, um—" Stephen rubbed his forehead awkwardly. "I fig-ured I could talk to you about this because, well, I didn't know who else I could tell."

Despite himself, Bryan was intrigued. "Tell what?" he asked, leaning forward in puzzlement. The quietness of the empty library added an air of conspiracy to their hushed voices.

"It's—" Stephen pushed his chair back from the table, as if trying to shove away his difficulty in finding the right words. "Hell, for a long time I thought I was just going crazy." He was still rubbing his brow, as if the thoughts were making his head hurt. "But then, last night . . . I saw something, last night. Down by the train station. I know I saw it."

He broke off, and studied his own fingers for what felt like a long time. Then he suddenly looked up, and met Bryan's eyes.

"I saw him, Bryan. I saw the Dark Man."

FOR THE FIRST FROZEN MOMENT, Bryan was trying to work out if this was some kind of sick joke, some way to embarrass and humiliate him for the story that he'd told the police so long ago and refused to ever retract. But what was the sense in that, so long after?

Stephen apparently took his silence for disbelief, or else now that he'd pushed himself into starting to talk, he couldn't stop. He went on, stumbling slightly, eyes fixed on the desktop as if he didn't want to look up and see what Bryan might be thinking.

"It's this town . . . there's something. There's something *wrong* here, and nobody ever sees it. Except I think maybe they all know about it really, and they just pretend they don't. There—hell, I don't know." He shook his head angrily. "Things . . . things are *off* here. I haven't always lived in Redford. We moved here two years ago. My old town was never like this." He rubbed his forehead again, a nervous gesture. "It's like . . . people are afraid all the time. Maybe not afraid, but . . . edgy, kind of. Like they never know when something nasty might suddenly happen to them. And things *do* happen here." Stephen risked meeting Bryan's eyes for a brief second. "Like what happened to your brother."

Bryan said nothing. He knew all this, of course—had thought it often enough—but this was the first time he could remember anybody else actually saying it out loud. If you could call hushed whispers in an empty library loud.

Stephen sighed, letting out air in a rush. "It started . . . well, if I'm honest, it started as soon as I came here. At first I thought it was just . . . a new place, you know. Kind of creepy, getting lost, not really knowing anybody." He gave a slight laugh without any humor in it. "Couple of times—more than a couple of times—I ran home like the Road Runner on a speed trip, but if you'd asked me I couldn't have told you what I was running from."

Bryan knew that feeling. Except he didn't run home, he just ran. Maybe once home had felt safe to him, but not any longer.

"Anyway, I started thinking it was me," Stephen continued. "Paranoid or something. But last night . . ." He sighed, and when he finally spoke again, his voice was almost a whisper. "I didn't imagine last night."

Bryan leaned forward, chest tight with a kind of nervous curiosity, and touched the sleeve of Stephen's shirt. "What did you see?" he asked softly.

Stephen leaned back in his chair. "I was walking home with my sister from her swimming lesson—I always have to walk her places, she's only nine—and I stopped to get a drink

8

from the station shops. Anyway, I came out, and all of a sudden it just seemed like the whole place was deserted, and I couldn't see Nina anywhere." He looked embarrassed. "I kind of panicked a bit." He let out a huff of breath and shook his head, as if making sure to mock himself before anybody else could. "Dumb, I know."

"It's not dumb," Bryan said very softly. Thinking of Adam. This time it wasn't embarrassment that made Stephen quickly pull his gaze away as their eyes met.

"Anyway." He swallowed awkwardly. "So I was getting a bit more panicked than I probably should have, and I saw something move around the corner—You know where I mean? That bit of grass round the back where there's a load of old bricks and stuff."

"I know it," Bryan agreed quietly. He had little call to go to the station now in any case, but that small expanse of neglected wasteland had that feel. That feel that said this was one of the Dark Man's places, and you might want to think twice about stopping to linger. . . . "I don't go back there," he said.

Stephen licked his lips nervously. "So yeah, I saw something move . . . round there. I . . . well, I thought it was Nina. Except at the same time I knew it wasn't, but I had to go and look anyway, and . . ." He paused. "And I walked around, and it was like I could feel the air getting *thicker*, and then I turned the corner and there was this, this *shadow*—"

He rested his forehead against the heel of his palm for a long moment. "I can't . . . Now that I'm telling you this, I actually didn't see much of anything. But he was *there*. Not just around, like he always is, but actually *there*. It was like . . . like having every shiver you've ever had, all at once."

Bryan spoke up, for what seemed like the first time in hours. "But he didn't get you," he said.

Stephen breathed out. "No. No," He repeated more firmly. "I was—it was like I was hypnotized, I was gonna keep walking forward even though I knew I had to get out of there, and then—" He shrugged, breaking the mood. "And then, you know, this guy comes walking around the corner all 'Hey, kid, your sister's looking for you.' And he was just *gone*."

"I don't think he can do . . . whatever he does . . . to adults," Bryan said slowly. "He can make them . . . not see things, forget things, but he can't . . . do things right in front of their eyes."

"He gets you alone," Stephen said softly. "Lures kids off alone, and then—"

"Yeah." Bryan closed his eyes briefly and tried not to see Adam, skipping confidently down the trail of stones without a thought for the power he was deliberately invoking. Adam, all alone in the woods with only Bryan to see what happened to him.

And Bryan hadn't helped. He hadn't done anything.

The school bell suddenly rang out, startling them both. Stephen laughed at his own nervousness, but Bryan couldn't relax enough to do that. Suddenly the library felt entirely too empty to be safe.

"Let's get out of here," he said.

Bryan didn't see Stephen for the rest of the school day, but he was waiting by the gate at half past three. "Hey. Mind if I walk with you?" he asked, a little sheepishly.

"No." Bryan shrugged. Maybe company would help a little; a distraction from the constant counting of steps. "Where do you live?"

"Wintergreen Avenue."

Bryan felt a shiver crawl across his shoulder blades. "Down by—"

"Down by the park, yeah." The park that led into the woods. His own house was little more than five minutes away, but Wintergreen was right within shouting distance.

Something in Stephen's tone, and memories of their hushed conversation that morning, prompted Bryan to speak aloud the childish words that jumped into his mind. "That's . . . a bad place."

Stephen stopped suddenly and looked at him sharply. "You know about those? I mean . . . I thought it was just me."

They started walking again. Yes, Bryan knew about those. It wasn't just Adam's disappearance that had soured the park and the woods for him. There was a feel to the air, a sense you couldn't quite describe of shivers down your spine, that told you when you were in one of the Dark Man's places.

"The park and the woods . . . that empty old house on King's Hill," he supplied.

"And that scrap of land down by the train station," Stephen completed. "Yeah. Yeah, I know all those places. I don't know what it is, but . . ."

"You can just . . . feel it," Bryan finished, and Stephen nodded silently.

They walked on for a few moments in contemplative silence. It was a midafternoon, Friday, the early days of July. The streets should have been alive with people sunbathing and tending their gardens, schoolchildren tumbling home in noisy packs. But as they turned off the High Street onto the side road that led towards both their homes, there might not have been another soul in the whole world.

There was a kind of oppressive stillness in the hot air; no wind stirring, no birds rustling in the trees. It felt like they were walking through a photograph, a snapshot of the streets frozen in time while the rest of the world went on without them. The hairs on the back of Bryan's neck started to stand up.

"Electricity," breathed Stephen suddenly. He was right; it felt like there was electricity in the air, a thunderstorm waiting to break.

The sun seemed to momentarily dim, as if a shadow had passed overhead. Bryan's head snapped up, but there was nothing in the sky—not even a cloud.

Neither of them said a word, but they were walking faster. The words of the rhyme started up in Bryan's head, defying his attempts to shove them back down again. *One in fire. Two in blood. Three in storm. Four in flood.* He half scuffled a step, trying to break the rhythm, but it didn't work and it was nearly enough to snap his nerve and start him running.

Five in anger. Six in hate.

He didn't want to run. It was like being in some stupid movie, being stalked by the beast. As long as you kept moving nice and slow, you were safe. But when you lost it and you started to run, it started to chase.

Seven fear. Evil eight.

In the movies, they always started running—like they always opened that door, the one that led to the cellar or the attic or the laboratory or wherever it was the monster was hiding this week. And down in some part of him Bryan knew why. It was crazy, it was stupid, but you *had* to.

Stephen's hand suddenly snaked out and tightly gripped his wrist. And that was it. Bryan started to run, dragging the other boy alongside him. They hared down the road like little children running from the scene of some infantile crime, but there was no one on the street to stop and point or laugh. Bryan thought that if they stopped and started hammering on doors to be let in, nobody would answer them. They wouldn't be there, or they just wouldn't hear.

People were good at not hearing things in Redford.

They were running alongside a house with a tall hedge, a neatly clipped bit of topiary, except that suddenly it seemed far, far taller than before, black and twisted and filled with threatening thorns. And the road was getting narrower, which was impossible, because it was an ordinary residential street with cars parked on both sides of the road. Only it wasn't quite a street anymore, but a narrow pathway between two huge hedges, like the path of a maze but with no side turnings to escape down.

There were no more cars, suddenly, and if the houses were still there they couldn't see them. But there was *something* behind that hedge, oh yes, something huge that snuffled and snorted as it ran. And it was as fast as the boys, faster, ready to burst through that hedgerow at any moment and throw itself at them.

The shadows cast by the monstrous hedgerows were so deep and dark it was midnight down between them. Bryan could see the faintest glimpse of light up ahead, an end to this tight dark passageway. But the hedges were growing closer together, no trick of perspective but actually moving closer together, closing in on them.

Bryan tripped on something, would have gone down, but

Stephen was still running, pulling him forward. Bryan could see the light before them growing, getting nearer, but that was just a cruel trick, wasn't it? A flash of hope to be snatched away at the last moment.

The thing in the hedges was coming for them. It was no longer outside, chasing and snuffling for a way to get in, but right behind them, on their heels. The thorns were wrenching and tearing at them, now, trying to hold them back for just those few moments, that matter of seconds that would allow the passageway to close in on them completely.

But now the sunlight was directly ahead of them, spilling through the twisted branches like the first rays of light returning after an eclipse. Bryan wrenched himself free from thorns that suddenly felt like fingers and forced himself through the tight gap, Stephen right behind him . . .

They burst through onto a busy street, traffic swerving out of the way in an explosion of horns and swearing. They somehow threaded their way through without being killed and reached the sanctuary of the opposite pavement, breathless.

BRYAN'S HEART WAS JOLTING in his chest as if it had somehow come loose. He turned and looked back at the entrance they had just come out of. It was just an ordinary street; two cars wide with pavement to spare, hedges neatly cropped and not five feet tall at their highest. Traffic zoomed past regularly, and now he could see other kids from their school making their way home in noisy packs. It seemed crazy to think that it could ever have been silent and still.

"It wasn't real," panted Stephen, sitting on the gravelly pavement beside him.

Bryan looked down at his arms, left bare by his short-sleeved white shirt and lightly tanned. There were scratches all the way up, souvenirs of a fight with uncompromising thornbushes. "It was, and it wasn't," he answered.

They cleaned themselves up at Stephen's house. After the initial adrenaline burst had worn off, Stephen had been surprised to find that he too was covered in slashes and bruises, and both of them had hands thick with the kind of grime you got from climbing trees. Bryan supposed you could try to twist it all into some theory about hallucinations and the ordinary hedges they had passed in their headlong flight, but he wasn't stupid enough to believe it himself. When the Dark Man was around, he could make things happen. Just because the street had returned to normal afterwards didn't mean it hadn't been changed momentarily.

Stephen's house was empty, which eased Bryan's discomfort at being there a little. But while Stephen poured them drinks in the kitchen Bryan tried not to look at the family pictures clustered on the middle shelf. Brother and sister together in every one; no accusing gaps here. A family still whole and healthy.

They sat in the lounge sipping black currant juice, sweet enough to almost make him gag, but helping to ward off the shivers that had suddenly threatened to take him over. It was a time of day when, at home, he might have switched on the cartoons up in his room to keep him company, but the two of them sat and drank in silence, not really looking at anything or each other.

"Do you want to tell me about Adam?" said Stephen finally.

Bryan wasn't sure he did, but suddenly the words started tumbling out without waiting for him to hear about it. "It happened five years ago. It was in all the newspapers—but you weren't here then, were you?"

"I heard about it," said Stephen, sipping his drink. "My mum warned me about the woods—she told me a little boy had disappeared there once. I didn't know it was your brother

16

until somebody at school told me. They said how you'd always told everybody it was the Dark Man; they were kind of joking about it but not joking, you know?"

Bryan knew. Nervous giggles, like whistling past the graveyard, because of course you're not *really* scared. "I don't think he was the only one. I think it's been happening for years. Forever, maybe. Do you know about the Devil's Footsteps?"

Stephen frowned, dark brow wrinkling. "That's that children's game, isn't it? My little sister was always coming home singing it when she started at school here. How does it go? One in—"

"Don't say it!" Bryan stopped him with a warning grab of his arm, more desperate than he intended to be.

Stephen nodded quickly in acknowledgment, and licked spilled black currant from the back of his hand as it threatened to drip onto the carpet.

"Sorry. I mean . . . you can say it. It's probably safe. All the Redford children sing it, everybody plays. They have since back when my parents were kids here, and before that. But then there's the legend—do you know that?" Stephen shook his head.

"It's like saying 'Bloody Mary' in the mirror thirteen times," Bryan continued. "The legend goes that there's a real Devil's Footsteps, a pathway in the woods with thirteen steps, and if you walk along it and say the rhyme, the Dark Man will come."

Stephen had stopped drinking. "And you found it," he said.

Bryan was surprised by the deep sense of relief he got from telling the story he had repeated so many times as a child, and for the first time having it simply accepted as truth.

"We found it. I was ten, I—" He found it difficult to continue, pretended he was pausing to take a sip. "I was scared, and I chickened out. But Adam was two years older, and he was never scared of anything. Well, not when he was with me. Because I was his little brother, and he had to show me that he wasn't scared. He had to *prove* that there was no such thing as the Dark Man. So he said the rhyme, and—" He couldn't even try to disguise how much this was paining him now.

"And the Dark Man came," said Stephen soberly. "Did you see—I mean, of course you saw him—but did you really *see?*"

Bryan knew what he meant. He opened his mouth, but there was no way to articulate what he had seen, nothing any more useful in his vocabulary now than in the one that had been at his command five years ago. He had seen, and he had not seen. To the endless frustration of the police, there was no clear-stamped set of features he could match a face to.

He was a man, and he was . . . other things. Constantly shifting, and yet all of his images the same.

He was the man in the bus station with the creepy eyes who had frightened Bryan once. He was the clown at Adam's seventh birthday who hadn't been funny at all, but terrifying with his false smile painted on. He was the serial killer in the late movie Bryan had snuck out of bed to watch, and the grinning tiger in the picture from his mother's old book of folktales.

Bryan had glimpsed the Dark Man for a matter of seconds—less. But in that brief instant he had seen all those images and a million more. All the things that had ever frightened him, no matter how tightly locked away in his mind and forgotten.

"I saw . . . He was . . . It felt like I saw everything."

18

"The shadow of everything you ever saw," agreed Stephen darkly. "All the goodness squeezed out like water from a sponge."

And Bryan knew, if he had ever doubted, that Stephen really had seen the Dark Man himself.

There was a long silence.

"What happened?" Stephen finally asked him softly. Bryan could only shake his head.

"I don't know," he admitted, wracked with guilt. "I didn't see. The Dark Man came, and . . . and I just ran."

He could have said that he'd been expecting Adam to follow him, but that wasn't true. As soon as the Dark Man had risen up to claim his brother, he'd known that it was too late. And in those last few moments, Adam had known it too. Bryan hadn't even seen his face, but the imagined expression was burned into his mind anyway.

Adam had been so confident, so mocking and skeptical on the surface. But deep down, some part of him must have believed, some small voice of fear that he'd pushed aside in his hurry to show off in front of his brother. For a fraction of an instant, at least, he'd believed in the power of what he was doing.

And the Dark Man had answered the summons.

The sudden creak of the front door bled into the silence, making them both jump. Stephen pushed a shaky hand through his cropped hair, and laughed at himself. "Oh, that'll be Mrs. Cunningham with Nina," he said, standing up.

Bryan shot out of his seat. "Um, I should—"

"Nah, don't worry." Stephen brushed his concerns aside without understanding them. "Just ignore her. I do."

"Stephen?" The voice of a harassed-sounding woman called out from the front hall.

"Hi, Mrs. C.!" he called back.

"Oh, good, you're here. Sorry to have to rush off, darling, Becca's got her piano lesson in an hour."

"That's okay!" Stephen lowered his voice to explain for Bryan's benefit. "She collects Nina from school 'cause Mum's at work and I can't get down there in time." The local junior school was in the opposite direction to the seniors, and uncomfortably close to the woods. Bryan was glad he never had to walk over that way anymore.

The front door slammed, and a short, slightly chubby girl with long dark braids and a Woodside Primary sweatshirt came barreling into the room. "Hey—" She came to an abrupt halt as Bryan's presence registered. "Hello." She eyed him suspiciously, as if anybody found in the company of her brother ought to be watched very carefully in case they were dangerous.

Stephen tilted his head towards Bryan. "This is Bryan. Bryan? This is the brat. Unfortunately."

"Uh . . . hi," Bryan said awkwardly. His experience of hanging out with nine-year-old girls had pretty much ended when he was nine, and he hadn't exactly been interested then. He rarely talked much with kids his own age, let alone younger ones.

Largely ignoring him, Nina glowered at her brother, and immediately went on the attack. "What did you do with my CDs, *Stephen*?" she demanded.

"What would I want with your CDs?" he said, looking exasperated.

"I was looking for them all morning!" she complained indignantly. "I wanted to take my CD player to school!"

"Well, you didn't look very hard, then, did you?"

"I wouldn't have to look at all if you hadn't moved them!"

"Again, what would I want with your CDs?" He twisted to shoot a long-suffering look at Bryan. "She thinks I listen to boy bands." He rolled his eyes.

Not at all at ease in the midst of sibling bickering, Bryan only mustered an awkward smile.

Obviously deciding that current company didn't require best behavior, Nina leaned over the arm of the settee to punch her brother in the shoulder. "You're always messing with my stuff!"

"You're always leaving your stuff all over the house!" Stephen retorted.

"Oh, so you *did* move them," she said triumphantly.

"I didn't touch your stupid CDs! Dad probably cleared them away before he went to work, you always leave them out of the cases so the undersides get all scratched—"

Nina glowered at him, unimpressed. "I know it was you," she said darkly.

Stephen let loose a heavy sigh, and looked across at Bryan. "Like talking to a brick wall," he observed, and pushed himself upright. "Come on, Bryan, unless you want to listen to another four hours of this."

His sister pouted at this abrupt dismissal, but stomped off up to what was presumably her room. Bryan heard the echo of a loudly slammed door, something that hadn't been heard in his own house for years. In the Holden family home, everybody shuffled around like the living dead.

Stephen sighed again as they headed out into the front hall. "Sorry about that, she's—you know." He twirled one finger close to his forehead in the gesture for "completely nuts."

"Yeah," Bryan said uncomfortably, more an empty sound

than agreement. "Listen, I should probably, you know, get back." He let the suggestion that his parents would be missing him hang unspoken, because that way it wasn't really a lie, was it?

"Yeah, okay. See you—whenever, I guess." Parting was made awkward by the strange circumstances that had jammed them together.

Bryan took a few steps backwards. "Okay. See you, then." He turned and hovered self-consciously in the doorway for a moment, then turned and started jogging towards home.

THAT EVENING THE HOUSE SEEMED COLDER and emptier than ever. His mother said nothing about his coming home an hour later than usual—perhaps she hadn't even noticed. He finished all his homework despite the fact that it was Friday, and went to bed early. He usually did. The faster he could get to sleep, the sooner the morning would come, and then he could escape.

When he finally fell asleep, his dreams were different.

In the winter months, it wasn't uncommon for him to go weeks at a stretch without knowingly dreaming, and to remember only scattered, nonsense fragments when he did. In the summer, though, it was always exactly the same. Not even a dream, but a memory; Adam's cheerful taunts and teasing as he went to his doom. The only thing that ever changed was the face the Dark Man happened to be wearing that particular night.

But this night, things *did* change.

He was still in the woods—everything came back to the woods, sooner or later—but he felt older, somehow; the teenager he was now instead of the little boy he'd once been. He looked down and saw his familiar body, still wiry and not quite full-grown but not quite a child anymore either.

And it wasn't Adam at his side. He was conscious of others behind him, though his body wouldn't turn to look. He felt instinctively that Stephen must be there.

And it wasn't Adam who stepped up to the rock pathway, but Bryan himself. *What am I doing?* he wondered. *No, stop!* But it was as if his body didn't belong to him.

The others behind him began to chant, and against his will his voice joined with theirs. The echoing sound was eerie, like little children gathered in the playground, and yet at the same time more adult, like a congregation joined in prayer.

One in fire. Two in blood. Three in storm. Four in flood. His feet were taking the steps, following the chant. Inside his mind he was trying to fight, but his body continued as implacably as if he were a robot programmed to move to the rhythm.

Five in anger. Six in hate. Seven fear. Evil eight. How had he not stopped on seven? "Fear" was the step for him, surely, for it was all he could feel, thickening the air, tightening in his heart. He tried to slow his heart rate but his body wouldn't obey the message his mind was sending it. He was utterly helpless, completely outside of his own control.

Nine in sorrow. Ten in pain. Eleven death. Twelve life again. And then there was no time left to struggle. *Thirteen steps to the Dark Man's door.*

Won't be turning back no more.

24

This time, the scream that jumped to his lips on waking was not his brother's name, but a wordless sound of sheer terror. This was not a repeat of that past horror, returning again and again to haunt him, but a premonition of a fresh new terror, still to come.

Something had changed. Something had been changed, and he thought it had happened because of what he and Stephen had shared the day before. The Dark Man's attention had shifted.

He was the target now.

Sweating but still chilled, Bryan rolled out of bed and padded down to the bathroom. It was early yet, but already bright. He had to squeeze his eyes shut against the flood of sunlight when he pushed aside the bedroom curtains.

The tight feeling of dream paranoia remained in his chest instead of fading. His skin prickled with the sensation of being watched—and he didn't think it was entirely imaginary. The Dark Man had *noticed* him yesterday, in a way that he hadn't since five years ago, perhaps not even then. What did a force so huge and so powerful care for one small boy who had witnessed his brother's snatching?

But in speaking with Stephen, he'd somehow changed that. They'd broken the code of silence that infused the whole of Redford . . . and the Dark Man had reached out, as if lazily swatting at a buzzing fly. They'd outrun his influence last time, breaking through into a street where there were just too many people passing for even him to divert—but what if he tried again?

Lost in such pessimistic thoughts as he mechanically chewed his breakfast, Bryan jumped out of his skin when somebody knocked. It was too early for the Saturday post, and nobody else ever came calling. He wondered if his father had locked himself out—he would go out walking sometimes, disappearing for hours without word of where he was going or why—but no, there he was, slumped in front of the TV. Bryan went to the door.

It was Stephen. Looking almost unfamiliar with his school uniform swapped for faded jeans, he seemed awkward and slightly embarrassed to be there. "I'm sorry, it's early, I just—"

"It's okay. I was up." Bryan cut him off. He was already dressed, ready to run out of the house as quickly as his morning rituals would let him. "Hold on a second. I'll come out."

The polite thing to do would be to invite Stephen in, but he didn't think he could quite cope with that. As he ducked back inside he automatically pushed the door until it was almost shut, as if the dark atmosphere that ruled his home now were something Stephen might be able to see if he looked in on the hallway. Bryan returned to the kitchen and picked up his keys.

"Dad, I'm going out." His father nodded vaguely. "With my friend Stephen," he added, wondering if that might get a reaction. He didn't hope for anything so outrageous as a conversation; maybe just an "It's nice you've made a new friend" or even just a quick "Have fun." Of course, it didn't happen. Just another disinterested nod.

Bryan's half-eaten cereal went down the sink, and that didn't get a comment either. His parents no longer nagged him about chores or eating right or even staying out late. He would have thought that the latter at least would have worried them, struck some chord of fear, but it was as if they had used up so much pain and worrying after Adam disappeared that they didn't have any left for him anymore.

The kids at school would think he was crazy if they knew he got jealous just listening to them complain about how strict their parents were, he thought as he let himself out to join Stephen. Anything, *anything*, would be better than this. He sometimes wanted to scream and shout and say outrageous things to make his father angry enough to yell or even hit him, but he didn't dare. He didn't dare; after all, what would happen if he did all that and they still just nodded and grunted as if he weren't there?

"Sorry about that," he said, pulling the door shut with a flash of relief that he felt guilty for. "My parents aren't—they aren't ready, this time of the morning." *They aren't ready for anything anymore.*

"Sorry," said Stephen again. "I know it's too early, it's just—" He shook his head. "After what happened yesterday, I couldn't just, just sit at home and watch TV and play music like everything was still normal. I just . . . had to get out of the house, you know?"

"Oh yeah, I know." Bryan could have laughed . . . if there had been anything remotely funny about it.

THERE WAS NO CHILL to the air even this early, but Stephen tugged his jacket closer about him uneasily. "I didn't know where else to go," he confessed. "Nothing's open this early, and I didn't want to stay out on the street, and my friends . . . well, they like to hang out in the woods."

Bryan nodded. "I usually go to the library." It was as good a place as any to hide; never too empty on a Saturday, and well removed from the Dark Man's most threatening haunts.

He and Stephen took a slow walk down to the local shops. The streets were quiet, but not in the awful oppressive way they had been yesterday. This was a safe, normal, early-morning quiet—few people on the streets but the occasional car swishing past.

They had to cross the bridge by the rail station along their way, and Bryan noticed how Stephen almost unconsciously speeded up as they were passing the steps that led down to the platform.

"I wonder why," he said thoughtfully, once they were well past it.

"Why what?" asked Stephen. They had been walking in a not uncomfortable silence until that point.

"Why that bit of scrap land by the station? There's nothing there." It was strange. In all these years he'd just accepted the Dark Man and his ways as solid fact, unchangeable, unavoidable, but now that there was someone he *could* talk to about it, he found that questions had begun bubbling to the surface. "I mean, I know about the woods, and that house on King's Hill . . . Well, there were always stories about that place."

"I heard some guy hanged himself," Stephen volunteered, and Bryan shrugged.

"Maybe. But I'm saying . . . it makes sense he'd be powerful there if it's some kind of haunted house or something. And the woods . . . well, yeah." He didn't want to talk any more about that right now. "But why behind the station?"

Stephen frowned and shook his head helplessly. "I don't know. It's just . . . How can it *be* like this?" he burst out suddenly. "Kids disappear all the time. And nobody even notices! Nobody stops and says, 'Hey, that's not right, that can't be normal.' Nobody says *anything*!"

"Sometimes I think they notice," said Bryan. "They notice, but they just pretend it's not happening."

"I hate this town," Stephen said softly.

The library was just opening for the day as they reached it; the only people there were an old man scowling at the rows of large-print books and a teenage boy hunched over stacks of newspapers for what was probably a school project. Bryan and Stephen walked past them both to a safely secluded table in the far corner.

"We should look this stuff up," Stephen said abruptly.

"Huh? Look what up?" Bryan asked.

"You know . . . the train station and everything. There must be books about the history of the town somewhere."

"I guess." Bryan had never even tried looking up the Dark Man's history; he couldn't imagine that any of it would have been written down. But maybe there was at least some clue to why that piece of land behind the station might belong to him. "I'll ask the librarian."

He half expected to get some outraged or shocked reaction; amazement that he was breaking the Redford code of silence. But she just pointed out the right shelf, as if it had been any other innocent request. "Are you boys working on a school project?" she asked him.

"Something like that," Bryan said.

"It's nice you've got a friend with you for a change," she added with a smile. And it struck him then that this woman, who didn't even know his name though she saw him every week, was probably more concerned about him than either of his parents. Neither of them ever noticed that he spent all his time alone.

The books she had pointed out were in the corner where the older boy had been seated. He'd disappeared somewhere—perhaps into the basement to get more newspapers. As Bryan passed his desk, he glanced at the binder left open on the tabletop.

It was open to a list of names, each with a month and

year beside it, and another number. It took him a moment to realize that they might be ages, because the highest value he saw there was sixteen.

He shrugged, and was moving away when one of the names suddenly penetrated. He scanned the list again and found it: Jeanne Wilder. The date was April of that year, and the age was fifteen. He suddenly recalled a MISSING poster fixed to the doors of the shopping mall in town—posters that were all too common in Redford—and . . . hadn't the name beneath the slightly fuzzy enlarged snapshot been Wilder?

Suddenly feeling chilled, Bryan carefully turned back the pages of names. Last year. Three years ago. Five years ago . . .

And there it was. Adam Holden. Twelve. And beside the letter "A" of his name was an asterisk in blue ink. There were several such marks, in different colors of ink, but the vast majority of names carried only blanks or penciled question marks. He wanted to see the key to understand what the marks might mean, but of course these were somebody's private notes and there wasn't any such thing.

He turned back pages with increasing speed. 1990. 1980. 1970. 1960. The lists started to grow sparser, and petered out entirely towards the early quarter of the century; was that when it started, or just when they didn't keep records of missing kids? Redford must have been a whole lot smaller back then.

All those decades of disappearances. Yet nobody ever seemed to notice. . . .

He frowned down at the binder. Apparently somebody had noticed.

Bryan turned back another page, and found himself at the front; a sticker in the top left corner of the first page proclaimed the binder to belong to "Jake Steinbeck, 11DCa," the way all his own schoolbooks and binders were labeled but the year had been scratched out.

A plastic wallet inside the cover was stuffed with dog-eared photocopies; the one on top was a road map of the town. Both the woods and King's Hill were marked with asterisks—the woods, of course, in blue to match the star by Adam's name. A wavy green line had been drawn around an area encompassing the station, as if the person drawing it had not been entirely sure where the third mark ought to fall.

Somebody cleared their throat, and Bryan jumped as if he'd been caught sneaking a look at something dirty. The owner of the folder scowled down at him darkly. He was taller than Bryan by half a head—judging by the scratched-out form number written in the binder, he was probably seventeen and out of school—with spiky black hair and a faded sports jacket. Bryan fought a sudden urge to say, "Mr. Steinbeck, I presume?"

"See anything interesting?" the boy challenged. There was a kind of "go on, I dare you" note in his voice, and Bryan suddenly thought that maybe this boy was thinking the same thing he had when he was talking to the librarian. Wondering if somebody was going to take issue with him for peeking into Redford's darker corners.

And that moment of recognition prompted him to take a chance. "Plenty," he replied, and tapped the photocopied map. "It's there, by the way."

"What?" Sullen aggression melted into confusion.

"The third site. It's that little overgrown patch behind the station. I guess it's harder to pinpoint because if kids disappeared there, people would just think they left town. But I'll bet some have died there."

Bryan looked up to see the boy wearing the exact same expression of shocked surprise that he himself must have worn when Stephen had first mentioned the Dark Man.

～ VI ～

BRYAN REALIZED THAT STEPHEN HAD COME over to join them. The boy twisted around to look at him a moment and then turned back to Bryan, his face contorted in almost comical confusion. "Who *are* you people?" he asked.

"This is my friend Stephen, and I'm Bryan. Bryan Holden." He saw the other boy's brow wrinkle in semirecognition. "Adam Holden's brother."

"Oh." The confusion quickly cleared, and the boy emptied out the folder of photocopies to riffle through it. He flattened out a newspaper article on the desk, and the other two leaned in to look at it.

The article Bryan didn't recall, but the photograph was a punch to the gut. It was that school picture, the last one they had taken together. He and Adam seated together on the bench in front of the cameraman's backdrop, Adam more smirking than smiling, and the picture not showing how he was half twisting Bryan's arm behind him to try and make him wince.

Bryan looked away for a moment, caught by the sting of tears that could still hit him from time to time. Then he walked the emotion back up inside where he usually kept it, and made himself read the article.

It had most of the facts right . . . so far as it went. It said Adam and his brother had been playing together in the woods when the older boy had been snatched. According to the article, Bryan had described his brother's assailant as "a dark man"; possibly, the newspaper speculated, a black man, or a dark-haired man in dark clothes. There was no mention of the Devil's Footsteps.

The words "Redford woods," "missing" and "dark man," had been highlighted. "It's rather a familiar story," said the older boy soberly. "I'm Jake, by the way," he added as an after-thought. "Jake Steinbeck."

"I know," said Bryan absently, still reading.

"You do?" he asked sharply.

"It's written on the inside of your binder."

"Oh." Jake looked taken aback for a brief moment. "Uh . . . Okay."

"Why are you collecting this stuff?" Stephen asked him. Bryan lowered the newspaper article and raised an inquiring eyebrow in support.

Jake sat down on the corner of the desk. "I had a friend . . . her name was Lucy Swift. Not many people knew her as well as I did. She used to get into trouble—smoking and drinking and that sort of thing—but she was never the kind of girl people thought she was. She was really smart, too." He paused for a long moment, then looked at Bryan sharply. "Everybody said she must have run away from home. And they're *wrong*. I knew her. She would never do that. She disappeared a year ago, and nobody ever knew any more about it."

"Seems like that happens kind of a lot around here," Stephen noted darkly.

Jake looked up at him earnestly. "That's not the half of it." He tapped his folder of data. "I've been looking, and I've been listening, and . . ." He paused. "Kids disappear here. I mean, *lots* of them. One every couple of months—if it's that long. And I know there are plenty of things that can happen to kids, but these ones vanish. *Totally* vanish. There are decades' and decades' worth of kids that have gone missing, and not one of them was ever found."

"That's because he took them," Bryan said, voice cool with controlled anger.

"The Dark Man?" asked Jake. Bryan nodded.

"Have you ever—" Stephen began to ask tentatively. "Have you ever, um, you know, *seen* anything?"

Jake frowned. "Seen . . . ?"

"The Dark Man," Bryan elaborated. "Did you ever see the Dark Man anywhere? Or anything else . . . strange. In the woods, or down by the station, or . . . anywhere."

Jake was shaking his head. "No. No—I've never seen anything like that. But I've heard . . . a lot of things that seem pretty crazy. And the more I read"—he looked down at his notes—"the more I think I'm starting to believe it."

"Believe it," said Bryan shortly. "This is real."

Jake hesitated, then got up and went to the bookshelf beside him. He pulled out a volume on local history and began to flip the pages. "I've read a lot of history books, but most of them don't have much about the legends. I think this is the best one, and even then . . . ah, yes, here we go." His attitude reminded Bryan of some of his more book-happy teachers; he suspected that reading and researching was something Jake had been accustomed to long before Lucy disappeared.

"What does it say?" asked Stephen, leaning forward.

"Not much. 'The Dark Man' . . . blah, blah, blah . . . 'local legend, akin to several mythological bogeymen. A stealer of children, never seen by adults, believed to haunt the Redford woods and prey on the unwary in the form of their worst nightmares.' I think that's all. : . . No, wait, there's more about the woods. Just a mention of the Devil's Footsteps legend—there's a version of the rhyme here."

"Don't say it!" Bryan and Stephen spoke together.

Bryan leaned in closer as the librarian shot the three of them a questioning look. "I think we're safe here," he said, glancing around and seeing that several more people had trickled in since their arrival. "But don't push it, okay?"

Jake was looking at them both with a thoughtful expression on his face. "You really do believe this, don't you?"

"We know what we saw," said Stephen firmly.

"Well, I don't," Jake pointed out. "Tell me."

So they told him; about Adam, about what Stephen had seen at the railway station, about what had happened the day before.

When they had finished, Jake looked at both of them carefully, as if trying to see if they were lying to him. Then he snapped his binder shut decisively, and said, "I want to go down to the woods."

"You don't," Bryan disagreed, shaking his head. "Trust me, you really don't."

"I have to see *something*!" Jake burst out. "I'm sorry, but I do. I'm not blind, I know something's at work here. And I know you believe what you're saying to me. But if you want me to believe it . . . I have to see it for myself."

Stephen shrugged, and looked expectantly at Bryan, who sucked in a deep breath, and then sighed. "Okay," he said. "Okay, maybe you're right. Maybe we should go looking for this thing, instead of letting it hunt us." His voice sounded steady enough to his own ears, but the idea made his flesh crawl. "Not in the woods, though," he added quickly. "Anywhere else, but not there."

"King's Hill," said Stephen promptly. "That empty old house. I've never been in it, but"—he shuddered slightly— "I swear, you can feel it just walking past on the street."

"Three people have disappeared there in the last few years," Jake told them. "Three that the papers knew about, anyway," he added. "Two boys went there in the middle of the night for a dare, and never came back. A toddler was snatched from the street in front of it while his mother was looking the other way."

"I bet there were more," said Bryan. "Kids who went there on their own, without telling anybody where they were going."

And now they were going to do exactly the same thing. Were they all completely crazy? A part of Bryan was definitely screaming so, but a lot of the rest just numbly thought, *Why the hell not? What difference did it make?* Better to walk right up to the Dark Man and say, "Go ahead and do it," instead of just cringing in terror, waiting. He'd never escape, so why keep running?

"So you think, if we go there, we'll . . . what? We'll see something?" Jake was trying not to be skeptical, but an edge of it was creeping into his voice anyway.

"I think so," Bryan said. He glanced at Stephen. "Yesterday . . .

we weren't even anywhere special. I think . . . I think maybe the fact we were talking about him, breaking the silence . . . That made him notice us. He could have gone after me a million times since what happened to Adam; obviously, he doesn't care too much about the fact I saw it happen. But when there were two of us, comparing notes . . . that got his attention."

But also, he thought, when there had been two of them, it somehow hadn't been quite so bad. Oh, at the time it had been as stomach-churningly frightening as ever, but afterwards it had helped just to have someone to say, "Whoa, that was scary" to. Because that was how you got over it, he decided. Shared it with somebody so that it wasn't just rattling around the inside of your skull until you couldn't tell if you'd imagined it or not.

"But *I've* never seen anything," Jake pointed out. "And I've been investigating the disappearances for months."

Bryan frowned. "Well, maybe if you're with us . . . Hell, I don't know." Something struck him as wrong in that, though. Some instinct that he couldn't quite explain was whispering to him that if Jake had never seen the Dark Man, then he shouldn't be noticing what he was, taking notes and making connections. If he couldn't see the Dark Man, then he should be like the others, looking the other way, somehow failing to notice the blindingly obvious.

Maybe Stephen was sensing the same thing, because he said, "Are you *sure* you never saw anything? Anything at all?"

"Well—" For a second, something in Jake's eyes made Bryan think he was about to share some story with them. And then he shook his head and just said, "No, nothing." He swept the binder off the desk into a black backpack, and zipped it shut with a decisive snap of the wrist. "Let's go to King's Hill."

⁓ VII ⁓

KING'S HILL WAS A STEEP INCLINE, difficult to climb but a roller-coaster ride to bike or skateboard down. Adam had always made fun of his little brother for being so nervous when they went coasting down it together, laughing at his fear of the slope. Bryan had never told him that it wasn't so much the reckless speed of the descent that bothered him as that empty house on the left-hand side, dark windows peering out like soulless eyes. He had always been convinced that one day they would be racing down, brakes useless, and something would come lunging out of that darkened house in front of him, leaving him no time to swerve out of the way.

Today he had no bike to recklessly coast down on. The one he had ridden when he was ten stood gathering dust in the shed, propped up beside Adam's oversized racer. Adam's bike had been so much too big for him that Bryan could probably ride it now, but the thought of taking it out himself made him feel physically sick.

He supposed that bike would stand there forever. His own might go, but his mother would never throw away anything that had been Adam's. His brother's belongings had all been boxed up, but somehow the boxes had never made it out of his room. Bryan never went in there. There was something horribly temporary about all those boxes, as if Adam had just that instant moved out and might be coming back any day now to collect his luggage.

The hike up the hill was as bad as he remembered. Jake, older and much taller, had the long legs to outpace him just walking, and the more athletic Stephen had no problem jogging to keep up with him. Bryan had done his share of running over the past five years, but that was a kind of terrified sprint, hotfooting it away from the things that lurked in the shadows. A sustained jog was not something he was good at, and the powerful July sun beating down did little to help.

By the time they got to the crest of the hill and the empty house came into view, Bryan's breath was wheezing in his chest more than a little. He should have been grateful it was downhill from there, but instead it felt as if he were being deliberately drawn towards the house, faster and faster, as if a spider were tugging him towards the center of its web.

The houses on King's Hill were not much different from those on his own street, falling somewhere in between the squalid estates and the "nice" part of Redford where the rich people lived. The houses were relatively old, from the thirties or forties, but mostly in good repair. They were all different, a pleasing change from the newer part of town, where the only variety in the rows and rows of terraced homes was what color people painted the front door.

Even in that mess of individuality, number 29 stuck out.

It had stood empty as long as Bryan had been alive; sometimes, he thought maybe it had been that way ever since it had been built all those decades ago. A forlorn FOR SALE sign was posted in the corner of the front yard. It didn't even have a phone number for the estate agent on it, as if whoever had planted it there had done it more to mark the house as empty than out of any genuine belief that somebody might want to live in it.

The house was a strange contradiction of disrepair and order. The gardens, front and back, were like jungles, but there were no discarded beer cans or heaps of other people's trash. The windows were unboarded, but none of them had been smashed. The brickwork was crumbling, but it had never been graffitied. Redford was a quiet town—at least on the surface—but even so such good behavior on the part of its youth was hard to believe.

It was an oddity—but, like lots of other strangenesses in this town, one that went completely unnoticed and unremarked.

Strange or not, there was nothing in the outward appearance of the house to account for the feeling like millions of tiny spiders crawling across his skin that set in as soon as Bryan saw it. "Feel that?" he said quietly.

Stephen nodded, tugging his denim jacket closer about him.

"It's just a house," said Jake. But Bryan thought he sounded a little uncertain.

They approached the front garden, Bryan's creepy feeling

growing steadily stronger. "What, do we just walk right in?" asked Jake in a low voice.

"Why not?" Stephen shrugged. "It's not as if anyone will see us do it." It was true; the street had become as eerily quiet as the one they'd gone down the previous afternoon. Hadn't there been a bunch of kids playing in their own gardens a few moments ago? Now there was nobody.

"How do we get in? Is there a window open round the back or something?"

"Try the front door," Bryan suggested. He had never been crazy enough to even contemplate going inside before . . . and yet he was somehow confident that the door would let them in. What good was a trap you couldn't get into?

He wished he hadn't thought of the word "trap." It brought to mind not some man-made device for catching unwanted pests, but a great, bloated plant like a Venus flytrap. A living thing, waiting patiently for its prey to come to it . . .

Jake stepped right up to the front door and pushed it, saying, "Don't be stupid, it'll be—"

The door swung open.

Bryan was suddenly very, very uncertain about this whole idea, but Jake had already stepped inside and he and Stephen just ended up following. Bryan couldn't tell if Jake honestly didn't sense anything amiss, or if he was putting up a mask to hide his own fears. That made him think of Adam.

And this is the same thing. We're doing exactly the same thing. Here he was again, trailing after someone who didn't really believe—or any rate, would rather walk straight into the arms of the Dark Man than *admit* he might believe.

And at that realization, Bryan would have stopped them and demanded they leave, if the door hadn't chosen that moment to swing shut without being pushed. Stephen jumped, but Jake just frowned and peered at the door. "It's on a latch," he said slowly. "It can't have been properly shut, or it would have been locked."

But Bryan's memory reported without hesitation that it *had* been shut, perfectly shut, shut tight against the door frame, and Jake wouldn't have had to use such a strong push if it had been standing ajar. And suddenly his need to get out was overwhelmed by a fear of trying the door. Because what if he tugged on the handle, and it wouldn't let him out?

Breathe, Bryan, he commanded himself. *If Jake can't sense the Dark Man, then you're safe with him.* After all, even the woods had been no danger to him when they were scattered with searchers. The Dark Man never haunted Bryan in front of anyone who wasn't sensitive to him.

But as Jake pushed past him in the entrance hall, brushing a strand of his dark hair away from his forehead, Bryan noticed a sheen of sweat on his face that hadn't come from the exertion of walking up the hill. He looked two skin tones paler than he had in the library, and Bryan couldn't help thinking that maybe he wasn't nearly as unaffected as he claimed.

"Let's just . . . let's just go through all the rooms and get out of here, all right?" Jake said quickly, and Bryan was in no mood to call him on his sudden nervousness.

There was a door to their left and Jake pushed through it into an empty room that looked far too big. *It's just the furniture, Bryan. It just looks big because there's no furniture.* There was peeling wallpaper on the walls, a pattern that was maybe flowers, maybe something else. But he couldn't tell, because it was too dark.

Windows. Where the hell are the windows? Bryan remembered the windows, knew their blank stare intimately. The room to the left of the front door had a huge picture window that should have flooded it with the morning sun. But this room had no windows—nothing but blank walls and that ancient wallpaper.

There was a click of a switch as Stephen tried it, but no flare of light. Bryan looked up to see if there was even a bulb, and the ceiling seemed to be about twenty feet above them.

Don't be stupid, you've seen the outside of the house, you know it's not that big.

Not that big on the *outside*, his mind corrected him.

Jake fumbled in his pocket, and yanked something out. It was a cigarette lighter, and it sparked into flame as he thumbed it. Bryan was too grateful for the sudden light to dwell on surprise that he carried it. Readjusting his mental image of Jake was the least of his worries right now.

The flame seemed tiny in the enormous room—and it *was* enormous now; twice the size it had been when they entered, he was sure. As if the walls themselves were shying away from the light.

In the suddenly dancing shadows, a splash of something dripped from above. *Damp*, he thought, *a leak in the roof*, automatically stepping away. Jake knelt down, bringing his lighter close to the floor to get a better look. *No, don't do that. I don't want to see*, Bryan almost said, but the words didn't come out.

A shallow pool of dark red liquid glistened in the light of the flame. Blood. As the three of them stared at it, another droplet landed in the pool with a barely audible splash.

∽ VIII ∽

"RUST," SAID JAKE, talking too fast. "There must be some kind of leaking pipe, with the rust turning it that color. . . ."

Stephen just mutely shook his head.

Bryan could see how Jake's hands were trembling in the way the fragile little flame danced as he stood and raised it to the ceiling. And how had he ever thought that the ceiling was high, that the room was big? It was as close and cramped around them as a coffin made for three, the ceiling almost brushing the spikes of Jake's hair.

The ceiling was yellowed, cracked, and bulging. And in the center, just above them, it was rapidly darkening with a spreading redness, blood leaching through from the floor above. Someone made a noise like a frightened animal. It took Bryan a moment to realize it had been him.

"There's someone up there," said Jake, a determined look

stealing over his face. "Someone hurt. It could be one of the missing kids!" He darted for the door before the others could grab him.

"No, wait!" Bryan snatched for the back of his jacket, only suddenly the room was room-sized again and Jake was out of reach.

"Lucy!" they heard Jake call as he dashed out into the entrance hall and towards the stairs.

And—were those stairs there a minute ago?

Not really aware of what he was doing, only knowing that he couldn't let Jake go up there, Bryan ran after him. He thought Stephen was on his heels, but he didn't look back to find out.

Jake was scrambling up the steps, and Bryan went up them two at a time after him. And even now, in the grip of extreme panic, the words came to him. *Two in blood. Four in flood. Six in hate.* He knew without even looking that there would be thirteen steps.

He caught Jake on the twelfth, grabbing him by the legs and forcibly yanking him backwards. The older boy flailed, smashing his hand against the banister, and Bryan would have lost his grip on him if Stephen hadn't been there to help seize him.

"What are you *doing?*" Jake demanded desperately, still struggling to get free of their grip. "Can't you *hear?*"

And suddenly, as if his words had summoned it up, Bryan could. A forlorn, failing voice, half calling for help and half just crying out in pain. "Lucy, it's me, it's Jake!" Jake yelled, but to Bryan it didn't sound like the voice of a teenage girl, not at all. It sounded more like that of a boy—a boy about twelve years old.

47

"Let me *go!*" Jake demanded, and Bryan felt so gut-punched by suddenly hearing that plaintive voice that he did let go.

"The step!" he blurted out before Jake could move on. "Not the thirteenth step!"

Jake spun around to face him, eyes dark with anger, as if he was about to yell something, but then he bit it off and used the banister to push himself up onto the landing without treading on the final step. Bryan leapt over it after him, not wanting to go up there and yet somehow needing to.

The first door on their left was bulging outwards from its frame, as if some huge creature was trying to force its way through the wood. Heedless, Jake grabbed the doorknob and tried to make it turn. It wouldn't.

"Hot!" he yelped suddenly, yanking his hand back. Bryan saw the dark metal knob already beginning to grow a dull red, like the rings on an electric stove top warming up.

The sounds of pain and distress from within were growing ever more frantic. Bryan tried to touch the door himself, but he couldn't even get his fingers near it—just forcing his hand through the hot air was like trying to plunge it into boiling water.

"Here!" Stephen pushed past them, wrapping the thick material of his shirt around his palm to shield it. He made a little moan of pain through gritted teeth as the heat sank through, but he didn't let go.

With a click like a gunshot, the door suddenly released, sending Stephen flying backwards as it opened. And suddenly, as if floodgates had been opened, water was rushing out around them.

Only it wasn't water. It took Bryan a moment to process

that it could be blood, because there was an impossible amount of it. It came rushing out around their legs like a high wave surging up the beach, horribly warm and with enough strength to nearly knock him down. He thought that if he fell to his hands and knees in it he might actually die.

And then it was draining away, pouring down the stairs with the thundering of a waterfall. Could one room have contained so much blood? Where had it all come from? Surely an elephant couldn't bleed that much if you drained it dry.

Something in him, the rational part of him, knew that, but the thick coppery taste of blood was clogging his nose and throat, making it impossible to think, to breathe. He didn't want to look inside the room, didn't want to with every bit of dread he had left, but he couldn't stop himself. *Nothing could be alive in there. Nothing could be alive.*

But something was. A small, weakly struggling figure hung suspended from a hook, a huge metal barb shoved through the flesh of its neck like a side of meat in a butcher's shop. Sneakered feet hung a few inches off the floor, blood still dripping down to pool beneath them.

So much blood. And it seemed to Bryan in that instant that the torrent of blood that had rushed past them had been nothing, meaningless, completely insignificant compared to the slow steady trickle from the neck of that hanging figure.

And it was strange. For a brief second it *was* nothing more than a figure, a vaguely human shape that his brain couldn't even begin to recognize. For a moment, he was even unsure what sex it was, what age. And then, as surely as an optical illusion becomes impossible to un-see once you've seen it, it was Adam.

Jake was shouting something beside him, only it sounded like "Lucy," and that wasn't right—couldn't he see that it was

Adam? Bryan tried to step into the room, not knowing what he could possibly do, only knowing that he had to get there, had to be with his brother. Why wasn't he moving? His body wasn't working. Something was holding him back.

He became aware that Stephen was shouting at him desperately, holding on to him and Jake as if they were wild dogs straining at the leash. What was he shouting? Were those words? Bryan couldn't hear anything, couldn't see anything but Adam.

Adam's eyes were fixed on his own. Impossible that there should be life in them, impossible that they should be anything but glazed, but they were fixed on him, hypnotic gray and full of pain and accusation.

Why are you letting this happen, Bryan? Why aren't you helping me?

And he was trying—he was trying to move forward but Stephen wouldn't let him. Bryan snarled something inarticulate, tried to wrench free but it just wasn't working.

Stephen's yells were beginning to crystallize into something a little like words, something Bryan could almost understand. Bryan hated him for holding him back, for shouting these words that were beginning to get in and distract him from the most important thing in the universe.

Thirteenth. He heard the word "thirteenth," felt an automatic chill slide down his spine, cutting through even his panic. *Adam.* But no, wait, that was Adam there, hanging there, *dying.* Dying because Bryan couldn't get to him. What did stupid steps matter against that?

Steps? What was that about steps?

Thirteenth step. Bryan, it's the thirteenth step. Don't go in there. Don't go—

"—in there! Bryan, Jake, can you hear me? Can you *hear* me?"

And then, like a bubble popping, the hanging figure wasn't a figure at all. It was a shadow, less than a shadow. He could still see it, but it was as if it were nothing more than a picture painted on a sheet of glass, placed in front of something else. Something altogether darker . . .

"I hear you, Stephen, I hear you!" Bryan's voice sounded hoarse to him, as if he hadn't used it for about a year. He realized that Stephen was practically crying with frustration and fear, trying to hold back the wildly struggling Jake, who was bigger and stronger than him.

Bryan leapt to his aid, helping to grab hold of Jake's arm and yank him backwards. Jake was crying too, yelling over and over again, "Lucy, I'm coming! Lucy!"

"Hear me! Jake, can you hear me?" Bryan found he was slapping the older boy round the face, not even conscious he was doing it. "It's not real, Jake, it's not real!"

Jake finally turned to look at him, eyes dazed with confusion. In that instant, as he looked away, the figure popped out of existence completely.

"What—?" Bryan thought he could see some sanity beginning to return to the dark eyes he was staring into, but he didn't dare wait around for it to happen. Who knew what else this cursed house might throw at them?

"Help me, Stephen!" Together, they hustled the older boy back down the stairs. This time, Bryan wasn't counting steps. He wasn't even aware of his feet touching them. They rushed Jake out through the front door, suddenly open again. It slammed behind them with a sound as final as the ending of the world.

THE SUNLIGHT OUTSIDE WAS AS BRIGHT AS EVER as they collapsed breathlessly in the front garden. Stephen was brushing compulsively at the legs of his jeans for several moments before he realized he was scrubbing at nothing. "What the *hell* . . . ?" He stared at his own fingers in complete bafflement.

"No bloodstains," Bryan realized, scrambling to his feet. He looked down at himself. "No *blood*." And yet he could still remember the horrifyingly warm red tide around his legs as the door burst open. . . . He stared at the others, heart still pounding. "Was any of that even *real*?"

"Some of it was." Jake thrust his upturned palm in front of them, the skin blistered with burns from where he'd grasped the red-hot doorknob.

"Oh, *ow*," sympathized Stephen, wincing in dismay.

There was the faintest of clicks from behind them, sounding as loud as a gunshot to Bryan's jangled nerves. They all whirled, to see the front door of the house slowly creeping open.

"It slammed," said Jake, an edge of panic creeping into his voice. "I saw it, it slammed and locked!"

"Let's get the hell out of here," Bryan said fervently. The acid taste of fear was back.

Stephen led the scramble for escape, but he stopped a few steps short of the pavement, looking dismayed. "Oh, no. Guys, can we . . . ?" He trailed off, realizing that staying in the garden was hardly an option. "Aw, hell." He resignedly slumped a few more steps forwards. "Okay, today is *really* not my day."

Running up the garden path after him, Bryan saw what had stopped him in his tracks: Nina, coming up the road in cycling shorts and an alarmingly pink top. There was no point hoping she hadn't noticed them.

"Hey! Brat!" Stephen yelled down the road, taking the initiative. "What d'you think you're doing? You're not supposed to be out on your own."

"I'm just going to meet Becca." Nina shrugged defensively. "Mum said I could."

"Yeah, and did you tell her where?" Stephen demanded, overprotective in the face of forcible reminders of just how dangerous Redford really was. "You're supposed to be *together* if you're going more than a couple of streets."

"God, she's only down at the shop!" Nina said, rolling her eyes incredulously. "What are you, my grandma? Anyway, what are *you* doing here?"

She eyed the three of them shrewdly, registering which

garden they were standing in front of. "Did you just come out of *Old Pete's house*? Oh, you are so dead," she said, starting to smirk. "Mum's gonna kill you if she knows you've been in there looking for ghosts."

"Nobody was looking for ghosts," Stephen snapped back, managing to muster more of a disbelieving sneer at the suggestion than Bryan would have been able to. "And who's this Pete guy supposed to be?"

She gave him a scathing look. "It's his house. He haunts it. Everyone knows that."

"Yeah, well, everyone's an idiot. And don't *you* get any ideas about going in there ghost hunting," he warned her. "Or I'll tell Mum you've been running round town on your own, and you'll be grounded, like, forever."

"*You* went in there." Nina folded her arms, clearly unimpressed.

"We had to get a tennis ball from the garden," Jake said, covering. She gave him the same skeptical once-over she'd given Bryan, clearly not reserving much respect for anybody who chose to hang out with her older brother.

"Where is it, then?" she demanded.

"We lost it in the bushes," Stephen said crossly. "Now could you just—?"

"What did you do to your hand?" Nina interrupted, looking at Jake.

He paused guiltily in the act of rubbing his reddened skin. "Burned it. This morning," he explained quickly.

"Hey, quit being so nosy," Stephen glowered, manhandling his sister away from the others. "Now, would you go bug Becca instead of me? We've got better things to do than babysit you all day."

54

"I'll tell Mum I saw you breaking into Old Pete's house!" she threatened.

"You won't, because you didn't, but I *definitely* saw you out here when you shouldn't be. And I'm the one with witnesses." He indicated Bryan and Jake.

Nina pulled a face. "Whatever," she sighed, outmaneuvered but unwilling to actually concede the argument. "But I'll still tell Mum unless you give me money to buy an ice cream," she added quickly.

Stephen glared, but dug in his pocket and dropped a few coins into her expectant palm. "That's all I've got, and you're paying me back when we get allowance," he warned.

"In your dreams." Having succeeded in twisting some money out of him, she skipped off quite happily.

Stephen shook his head as she left. "Sorry about that," he sighed. "Nosy little brat." He slid his hands into his pockets and looked at the others. "Where to now?"

"Somewhere other than here," said Bryan, with feeling. The sensation that the house was watching them was back with a vengeance.

They ended up going to Jake's house. He led them up to the attic, a surprisingly comfortable if low-ceilinged room with a skylight that let in a little sun. There were a few cushions and a stereo, though most of the space was taken up by haphazard piles of books. A Polaroid photo pinned to a beam showed a younger Jake and a grinning girl with strawberry-blond hair; Lucy, Bryan guessed.

"Sorry, I know it's a mess up here," Jake apologized, nudging papers aside with a foot to make space. "I'm not used to anyone else coming up. Me and Lucy used to sit up here and

55

smoke. Well, *she* did," he corrected himself vaguely. "I didn't, back then."

Bryan wondered if he'd taken it up as some strange way of extending Lucy's presence there a little longer. Not the healthiest way to cling to someone's memory . . . but then, who was he to talk?

It was strange, though. This was obviously a private hide-away that had been shared by Jake and Lucy, but there was none of the choking, oppressive feel that he associated with Adam's old room and the places where he could feel his brother's presence. He had a sense that they should feel like this; safe and full of memories, not somewhere where you felt as if the air was being sucked out of you and you were slowly strangling.

He wondered if Lucy Swift's old house felt like his own. Did her parents shuffle round like zombies and talk without really talking? Were there parts of the house that they never entered, rooms full of boxes that would never be taken away? Did Lucy have a little brother who felt like he was drowning in the silence where she used to be?

He pushed that line of thought away forcefully. It wasn't fair to act as if everything were down to his parents; it wasn't their fault that the house felt like a live-in tomb. It wasn't their fault that when Adam had disappeared, they'd somehow forgotten that Bryan existed too.

He shook himself out of it, and forced his mind back to King's Hill. "That house. It's like a Venus flytrap," he said aloud. "It lured us in, and it slammed the trap shut—but we got away."

"And then it opened up the trap again, waiting for the next happy little insect to come along," said Stephen darkly.

"Or for the same ones to be stupid enough to come back,"

Bryan said, thinking of that door creeping open. And hadn't there been, underneath that pinprick of returning fear, something else? Some tiny little desire, however well buried, to go back in? To walk back into the trap and see if you could still get away the second time around.

A pained look was beginning to creep over Jake's face. "It *was* her," he said quietly. "It was Lucy. I saw her!" He stared each of the others directly in the eyes, as if daring them to disagree.

"I know you saw her," Stephen said gently, "but it wasn't her. It wasn't her."

"But she—she was—"

"It was some kind of—Hell, I don't know, some illusion or something. It was him, the Dark Man, making you see what he wanted you to see."

"I saw Adam," said Bryan softly. And it was only as he said it that it first occurred to him that he had seen the Adam of five years ago, a twelve-year-old boy. If Adam was . . . if there was some crazy parallel universe where he could be alive now, he would be seventeen, nearly fully grown, not a kid younger than Bryan himself.

That helped him to figure out how to prove it to the unconvinced Jake. "What did she look like, Jake?"

Jake's forehead crinkled in a frown. "What . . . ? She just . . . she looked like Lucy. Like she always did."

"*Like she always did*," Bryan echoed pointedly. "*Think* about it, Jake. When did she disappear? A year ago? Did she look any older, Jake? Was her hair any longer? Did she look any fatter, any thinner? Any taller?"

"I . . . I . . . no," Jake said slowly. "She looked . . . just the same. Just the same as when she disappeared."

Bryan laid his hands on Jake's shoulders. "It wasn't real, Jake. What we saw . . . none of it was real."

In reply, Jake stretched out his hands palm upwards. "This is real," he said, nodding at his blistered right hand.

Bryan pushed back his sleeves to display the cuts he'd taken from his headlong flight past the hedges the day before. "So are these! I never said he couldn't hurt you. He can hurt you plenty! But he can also make you see things that aren't there, see anything he wants you to."

"D'you think this is . . . what happened?" asked Stephen slowly. "Did all those other kids see stuff like this, when he came to get them?"

"I'm sure of it," Bryan said darkly. "He . . . pulls stuff out of your head. What you're most afraid of, what you're expecting to see . . . He uses your nightmares against you."

Jake leaned forward pensively, resting his chin on a loosely cupped fist. "If that's true, then he must feed on the beliefs somehow, like some kind of a parasite. The legends, the chant . . . they must play directly into his hands. It's almost like a formula, telling you exactly what to believe. Keeping people afraid."

"Yeah, well, he's doing a pretty good job of it right now," said Stephen, a little shakily. "That thing scared the *hell* out of me." He wrapped his arms around his knees, the beanbag he was sitting on rustling as he shifted his weight.

Stephen, Bryan had noticed, wore his anxiety quite openly; he didn't avoid putting words to the things that had been unspoken constants of his own world for what seemed like forever. Maybe that was why he'd been the one to finally break the silence, and just walk up to somebody and say, "This is what I saw—do you believe me?" Bryan had spent so

58

many months talking to deaf ears about what had really happened to Adam, it would never have occurred to him to even try again.

"What did *you* see, Stephen?" It suddenly occurred to him to wonder.

Stephen shook his head slowly. "I—I don't even know. For a moment I thought it was . . . I thought I saw—" He stopped, looking distressed. "But then you both started yelling that it was Adam, that it was Lucy, and it was like it—it all collapsed in on itself."

"You broke out of the illusion," Jake realized. "Because . . . maybe it didn't know quite what to show to you. We both went in there knowing—expecting . . . the fear must have been right *there*, ready to pull out the instant we stepped into that room. But the Dark Man had to think more about you; he had to dig deeper, trying to find something that fit, and it took too long. He couldn't quite fool all of us with the same trick at the same time."

"So?" Bryan shrugged, a little too aggressively. His instincts hadn't quite caught up with the calmer surroundings, and he was still more than a touch on edge.

"So . . . we have power too," Jake continued. "It matters what *we* believe. The shapes he takes come from *us*, not from somewhere else. And if he uses our fears and our nightmares to shape reality, then in a way, we control him."

"Not much of a way," Bryan said with a grimace.

"I don't know about that," Jake said softly, twisting around to meet Bryan's eyes. "Because it seems to me that if believing he can hurt us makes it possible . . . then believing we could hurt *him* makes *that* possible. If our belief gives him power, it can take it from him too."

59

THERE WAS A LONG MOMENT OF SILENCE, and then Bryan
sighed tiredly. "Oh, come on. That's crazy. You can't just . . .
This isn't clap your hands and 'I believe in fairies.' It's not like
I can . . . I can pick up this pencil and say, 'This pencil has the
power to kill the Dark Man,' and it'll come true. It doesn't
work like that."

"I think it does," Stephen corrected him slowly. "Just not
with pencils. You've got no *reason* to believe in pencils. But if
everything the Dark Man does or shows comes from what he
takes from people's minds, then it has to have some kind of
influence over him. Maybe if there was something you *did*
have a reason to believe in—if there was some way we could
find out more about him . . ."

"*How?*" Bryan demanded, frustrated. "Nobody ever talks
about this stuff, even as a joke, even as if it was just a legend.
I should know."

Stephen rolled sideways on the beanbag to look across at Jake. "What about in books? You must have read, like, the whole of the Redford reference library by now." By the look of it, he had most of it still stashed there in his attic.

Jake shrugged awkwardly, as if embarrassed to be caught out in his research. "I've got history books, but . . . it's not as if I knew what I was looking for. I mean, before today I didn't even—" He laughed slightly nervously. "Well, I never saw anything like that before." He flexed his burned palm and looked down at it, as if it was the only thing still anchoring him to such unbelievable memories. "It's still pretty hard to believe it even happened, you know?"

Bryan wasn't sure he did know. All the memories from his early childhood seemed to run together and funnel any recollection towards that day in the woods five years before, until he could no longer remember what it was like to live without the Dark Man's shadow hanging over him.

Stephen eyed the piles of books, looking somewhat daunted. "So is this going to involve, you know, looking stuff up? Because, well, if you saw the mark I got for my last history project—"

"Wait a second." Jake leaned across him to scrabble for one of the books. "What was it your sister said they called the house? Because I think I might have read something about—" He skimmed through the index, then shut the book. "Maybe it was in this one. Hold on a second."

He flicked quickly through the pages with the attitude of one who did this all the time. Bryan, however, was still curious about how Jake could have been researching everything about this town for so long, and yet never come face to face with the Dark Man. How could he have been breaking the unwritten code of silence if he didn't really *believe* . . . ?

"You really never saw stuff before?" Bryan asked. "Not the whole time you were investigating?"

"Huh?" the older boy asked vaguely, attention firmly caught between the pages of his book.

"There must have been . . . well, didn't you ever see— feel . . . ?" Bryan wasn't sure he could articulate what it was like to be aware of the Dark Man's presence, conscious of him through all his senses like a thick and spreading pool of menace.

"Well . . . ," Jake said almost distantly, as if he was paying more attention to what he was skim-reading than what he was saying. "One time . . . I thought I saw . . . Ah." He abruptly snapped out of it and straightened up. "I knew I'd read this! See, King's Hill. The Pete's house thing jogged my memory."

Bryan and Stephen craned over the story eagerly as he swiveled the book their way. After a moment, though, Bryan sat back in disappointment. "It doesn't say much," he said.

"It wasn't much of a story," Jake agreed with a slight shrug. "But the rumors are true—someone did kill himself there."

"Peter Hayward," Stephen read. "Well, I guess that explains who Old Pete is supposed to be. But who was he?"

"Nobody important," Jake replied. "I mean, he worked in the old children's home, retired after it closed, and one day he just . . . hanged himself. Nobody ever knew why."

Stephen frowned. "Could Nina really be right about him haunting the place? I mean, if there actually *is* a ghost—"

"He didn't even *die* until well after the kids started disappearing," Bryan pointed out, shaking his head. "It's probably got nothing to do with him. It's just the kind of spooky story that gets passed around—he killed himself there, so people

62

say the house must be haunted. If the Dark Man takes his power from what kids are afraid of, he probably moved in as soon as the rumors did."

"There must be some *reason*, though," Jake insisted. "Why that house? Why Hayward?"

"Why not Hayward?" Bryan demanded. "Why me, why you, why him, why anybody? It doesn't have to make sense. It doesn't have to be *logical*." He felt the old well of bitterness spring up, and there was an awkward lull of silence. He irritably elbowed aside a pile of paperwork to rest his chin on his hands.

"Still . . . ," said Stephen mildly, a few moments later. "Why that plot of land behind the train station? So Old Pete was a real person, his house has a history . . . why down by the train station?"

"The station's new," Jake observed, nose already in another history book. "They only built it early last century." It apparently didn't occur to him that some people might not strictly call that "new." "They knocked down a lot of older buildings to make way for the railway—I remember reading about the protests. I don't know what used to be there, though, it may have been a factory or something."

"Maybe we should go and look," Stephen suggested softly. Bryan met his gaze in astonishment.

"Why—?"

"I want to find out what's going on, Bryan," he said seriously. "What if nobody had come round the corner when I met the Dark Man? What if it had been my sister? I need to know . . . why these places? Why Redford at all? I need to know whether we can stop it."

Bryan wanted to rant and scream about the hopelessness

of it all, but somehow, when he saw Stephen's earnestness, the emotion congealed into a nauseous lump in his chest, and he felt . . . tired. Not just tired from the day's events, but from the whole past five years. He sighed heavily. "Let's just—not today, okay?"

He pushed his hair back from his forehead. It was too long; when was the last time he'd had a haircut? His parents didn't think about things like that anymore.

He sighed again, knowing the others were looking at him; perhaps only imagining that it was accusingly. "Maybe we should go there—just . . . not today. Tonight. Whatever. What the hell time is it, anyway?"

Stephen checked his watch and stood up, swearing. "It's half past four—my mum's gonna kill me! Can I use your phone, Jake? I keep telling my dad I need a cell phone, but he never listens."

It would never have occurred to Bryan to badger his parents for a phone of his own. In their zombie-like state they'd probably have just paid for it without question, but what could he use it for? It wasn't as though he ever had anybody to call.

"Sure, it's in the living room, down that way."

They all stepped down from the attic, and Bryan blinked at the difference in the light level. His stomach twinged, and he only remembered then that he hadn't eaten anything but half a bowl of soggy cereal. Funny how sheer terror could wipe away your appetite.

They waited in the hall while Stephen made his call. He leaned around the door, trailing the phone cord, to look at them. "Hey, you guys want to come over for dinner? My mum says you can."

Bryan would have liked to refuse, but Jake was already

muttering about writing his parents a note, and Stephen had agreed and hung up before Bryan could think up an acceptable excuse. He decided he'd better call his own parents, though he doubted they'd miss him if he didn't come home. It took him a moment to even remember the number, he had reason to call home so rarely.

"Hello? Holden." That was his dad, he was glad to hear. It was easier to try and make conversation with his dad than his mother. Talking to her was like talking to a very deaf but polite old lady who would just nod and say, "Mm-hmm" to whatever you tried to tell her.

"Dad? It's Bryan." He didn't say "it's me" for fear of sparking a momentary belief that it might be a runaway Adam finally calling home.

"Bryan," agreed his dad, perfectly pleasantly, but more as if he were talking to a distant cousin than the son he saw every day.

"Um, I'm not going to be home for dinner tonight, okay? I'm gonna be round a friend's—my friend Stephen, I mentioned him this morning?" He was gabbling, like he always did. He hated the way he did that, just talked on and on into the silence as if filling it up fast enough would be the key to getting his parents to talk to him.

"Okay, son. See you tonight." And he hung up. Right about now, Bryan would have welcomed an interrogation—where are you going, what are you doing, when will you be back, why such short notice? Even if he'd phoned five minutes from dinner and a finished meal had to be scraped into the bin, he'd probably have got the same distant nonreaction. Because it was Jake's phone, he resisted the urge to throw the handset across the room and kick something.

"Your parents okay with it?" Stephen asked him, wandering back in.

"Oh, *fine*," said Bryan. He heard the bitterness twist in his voice, but he was powerless to prevent it.

Stephen looked uncomfortable, but he didn't say anything. What could he have said?

ANY HOPE OF PERHAPS HIDING up in Stephen's room to eat dinner was snatched away when the door was opened by a hearty man who was like a larger, more muscular version of his son. He clapped Stephen on the back, asked where he'd been and why he'd left so early, asked who his friends were, turned to Jake and Bryan and spoke to both of them. Bryan stretched his face into a smile that ached, answered politely, and wished he could just sink into the ground.

Inside the house, it got worse. Even the day before, when it had been just him and Stephen, he'd been conscious of the difference in the atmosphere, uncomfortable inside a house that still felt like a home. Bustling and full of life, it was a hundred times worse.

Mrs. Bacon was a petite and extremely energetic woman who flashed brilliant smiles at them as she busied herself preparing the meal and talking a mile a minute. "Stephen, get the spare chairs from the other room. Nina, do you have to do that when we have guests? Put the cat *down* and go and get ready for dinner. Where are the nice table mats? No, not those ones, dear, remember you burned a circle in one with the casserole? The other ones. Now, what did I do with that spoon—?"

Bryan flattened himself against the wall to keep out of the way, and wished he were somewhere else. The Bacon household seemed to be overflowing with noise and moving bodies, everybody scrambling around and talking over each other and getting in each other's way.

It was the picture of a chaotically happy household. It was hell.

"So, what have you boys been up to all day?" Stephen's mother asked them as they ate. It was a big meal, and beautifully prepared; Bryan was used to bland, stodgy dinners at odd times of the evening, overcooked or undercooked because his parents didn't bother paying attention. It added an irrational layer of guilt to enjoying the meal, and on top of his too-long-empty stomach, it was giving him indigestion.

Not used to being questioned about his day, he choked, fumbling for an answer, but Jake stepped into the breach. "We've been working on a history project. About the old Redford, what it used to be like before they built the station and the newer parts of town."

"For school?"

"Uh, mostly," Stephen said, apparently something of an awkward liar. He kept his eyes on his dinner in the guise of pouring more gravy on it. "It's, um, it's quite interesting, though."

Nina gave a disdainful snort at that, pushing her broccoli

around the plate as if it offended her. "What, looking at a bunch of old buildings? You should write about the ghosts."

"Nina." Her mother gave her a reproachful look, but the boys exchanged slightly anxious glances. Was she about to drop Stephen in it for their expedition to Old Pete's house?

"What ghosts?" Jake asked carefully.

Nina smirked wickedly at her glowering brother across the table, but shrugged as she took a quick gulp from her glass of water. "There are ghosts *everywhere* in this town. Marcie Holliday was down at the woods one time, and *she* saw—"

"Nina, not at the dinner table, please," her mother sighed. And that put a stop to the discussion, at least until after dinner.

"Who's Marcie Holliday?" Jake asked in a low voice as they left the table, Stephen's parents disappearing into the kitchen.

Stephen shrugged. "Some kid in Nina's class. You think it might be—?"

"I'll ask. Nina!" Jake called.

She turned in surprise at the foot of the stairs, long braids flying about her head.

"You're still going on about ghosts, then?" Jake asked.

She shot them all a highly suspicious look, but apparently the desire to tell her story won out over a chance to annoy her brother. "There *are* ghosts in the woods," she insisted, obviously expecting skepticism if not outright teasing. "Marcie saw them when she was down in the park with her dad."

"What did she see?" Jake pressed lightly. Bryan hung back to listen, unpracticed at prying information out of nine-year-olds. The places you were likely to run into younger kids were places he'd once gone with Adam, and visiting them now was a cold knife to the gut.

69

"She said they all came out of the woods," Nina said, arms still defensively folded across her chest. "And they were *really* creepy. They were all little kids—like, ghost-kids—coming to get her, and take her back with them. And *singing*."

"Singing what?" Jake frowned, although Bryan and Stephen had already exchanged a knowing glance.

Nina gave him a scathing look. "You *know*. The rhyme! The Devil's Footsteps rhyme. *One in fire, two in blood, three in storm and*—"

"You don't have to *sing* it, dummy." Stephen quickly cut her off, rolling his eyes pointedly. Nina made a face at him. She didn't repeat any more of the rhyme, but inside Bryan's head the singsong chant continued of its own accord.

Four in flood. Five in anger, six in hate, seven fear and evil eight . . .

"Oh. That." Jake laughed nervously at himself. "Right. So what happened?" he continued hastily. "With Marcie and the ghosts."

"She ran back to her daddy like a little girl," Nina said, with all the scorn for this childish behavior she could muster. "She's *such* a drip. If it was me, I'd have gone right back there with a flashlight and Dad's camera, and—"

"You stay *out* of the woods, Nina," Stephen ordered sternly, grabbing her by the arm.

She shook away from his grip in annoyance. "God! You're always the same, *Stephen*. I'm not a *baby*."

"Yes you are, you're a whiny little baby, and you know you're not allowed in the woods, so don't go down there. I mean it!" he threatened.

Nina heaved a deliberately theatrical sigh, and rolled her eyes. "What. Ever." She turned and stomped off up the stairs.

"Control freak!" she yelled down at him when she reached the upstairs landing, before disappearing into her room with a slam.

Stephen just shook his head and leaned back against the wall, casting his eyes heavenwards. For a moment he looked as if he was going to grumble about how annoying she was, but then he slid a guilty sideways look at Bryan, and didn't.

"So what do you think?" he said instead, after a moment.

"Ghosts in the woods?" Bryan shrugged. "Yeah, why not? Just another Redford tale," he said sharply. "Every kid sees stuff, and then they forget it as soon as they grow up. *If* they grow up."

"Not everybody does," Jake said quickly. "I mean—I never did." But there was something shifty in the way he said it—almost as if it was as much to convince *himself* he hadn't seen anything as to remind them. Bryan might have pressed him about it, but then Stephen spoke up, grinning.

"Never did what—grow up?"

They all laughed, feeling the tension flood out, and for a while, at least, things felt pretty okay.

~ XII ~

THEY HUNG OUT FOR A BIT at Stephen's house, trying not to think too much about the Dark Man. Bryan had spent plenty of evenings doing exactly that, but he wasn't used to having company in it. He felt strangely detached through most of it, as if he were watching himself from the outside. How had he come to be living a life where lying around playing computer games was an alien world, and fleeing the forces of darkness was everyday?

Although walking right into the house on King's Hill— that hadn't been exactly fleeing, had it? They'd still run away . . . but they'd broken the illusion before they had. And the next day they were going down to the train station to do the exact same thing again. Poke about in the hornets' nest, trying to find out where they were coming from, and how to stop being stung.

The ground had somehow shifted under his feet, now that

he had companions. He still wasn't sure their investigations were anything but useless—but before, it would never have occurred to him to make them at all. The past five years had been numb, unthinking acceptance, but now that the others were asking questions, he suddenly realized he wanted to know the answers as much as they did.

"So . . . how did you even start looking this stuff up?" he asked Jake as they walked home along Wintergreen Avenue. "I mean, was that after Lucy . . . disappeared, or . . . ?"

Jake shrugged slightly, hands in the pockets of his sports jacket. Bryan was struck by the way he could still talk about Lucy, hear her name without flinching. Jake was sad, and angry, and looking for answers, but Lucy had been taken *from* him; he hadn't abandoned her, he hadn't left her to die. Maybe that was how he could remember her without every trace of the good memories being eaten alive by the crushing guilt of what had happened.

"I don't know," he said slowly. "I mean, I was always interested in history. Most of those books up in my attic I already had. But after she disappeared, after everybody gave up and stopped looking . . . It became an obsession, I guess. I started going through the newspapers, tracking all the kids who disappeared, trying to prove . . ." He shook his head. "I don't know what I was trying to prove. Just trying to show all those . . . *idiots* . . . that they were being blind, that she wasn't just another teenage runaway." He smiled wryly. "Nobody listened."

"Nobody does," Bryan agreed, remembering. Nobody ever listened, and after a while, you stopped trying to talk.

"But the more I found out . . ." Jake breathed out slowly. "The more it just started to seem that no one could have ever looked at this before, because how could they not notice? How could anybody have ever looked at this list of missing kids and not seen . . ." He shrugged. "I don't know. It just seemed so . . . impossible. So I kept collecting it up, putting it together, and I started seeing the patterns . . . stories about the woods, stories about King's Hill . . . I started wondering if there was some kind of a cult or something. I mean, I knew about the Dark Man legend, of course, but—"

"But what?" Bryan demanded. He was sure Jake had to be hiding something—or at least denying something. How could Stephen, who'd only lived in Redford for two years, have come face to face with the Dark Man, while Jake, who'd grown up here, had never seen anything?

"Come on, Jake," he urged, trying not to sound accusing. "This morning couldn't have been the first time you ever saw anything. You grew up in Redford, for God's sake—every kid who's lived here has seen *something*." He remembered all the scenes from infant and early junior school; teachers smilingly chalking it up to youthful imagination as they comforted the kids who'd seen ghosts in the storerooms and trolls lurking behind trees. And then sent them right back out to play in front of the waiting claws of the Dark Man.

"Maybe that's true," Jake said, "but I swear, I've never seen anything." And Bryan would have been forced to leave it at that, except Jake quietly added, "It wasn't anything."

"What wasn't?" Bryan asked quickly.

"Nothing!" Jake insisted; angry, but at himself, not at Bryan. "I thought, one time—" He broke off, shaking his head. "But it was just me, I was scaring myself. It wasn't anything."

Bryan wanted to push him further, but made himself wait.

They walked on in silence, crossing at the corner of Geller Street. A few moments later Jake went on as if barely aware Bryan was even there.

"I saw this documentary once. I was pretty little—six, seven, I don't remember. It was about wolves. There were these white wolves, and they were . . . they were *beautiful*. Do you know what I mean?"

Bryan nodded, not wanting to interrupt the hesitant flow.

"I was totally mesmerized. I had a pet cat once, and I could watch him for hours, but those wolves were . . . something else. You wouldn't believe anything like that could exist in the world. They were like . . . gods. Animal gods. And they looked like ghosts, the way they moved. Totally silent, as if they weren't really there at all; as if the rest of the world was something they could just kind of melt through. As if nothing else apart from them was really real."

Jake was quiet for a long moment, and he and Bryan walked together in silence. Then he suddenly started up again. "I saw them . . . hunting. In the trees. I can't remember where it was, or what they caught. I just remember the way they appeared out of nowhere and tore it apart. And that little animal—I don't think it matters what it was, anything would have been the same. Nothing, nobody could ever get away from those wolves, those wolf-gods, because they were just too perfect."

Bryan noticed Jake glancing over his shoulder, almost automatically. He wondered if Jake realized he'd done it.

"I used to have nightmares," Jake continued. "I'd be in the woods somewhere, and they'd be there. Watching me, stalking me. And I'd see them; I'd catch little glimpses of them gliding between the trees. And then . . . and then they'd vanish. And you *knew.* You knew that as long as you could see them, you were safe, but once they disappeared . . ."

At first Bryan thought Jake had come to another halt, but instead his voice had dropped to an almost inaudible whisper. "And one time I thought I saw them for real. I was in the woods with my dad, and he'd just gone off to pick something up that he'd dropped. And I saw . . ." He shook his head angrily. "But it was just a shadow. Or, or, it was a dog or something. Somebody's husky dog. But just for a moment, just for a moment, it looked like a white wolf."

He fell silent then, and Bryan struggled for something to say. Inside, he was sure that the wolf Jake had seen had been real; as real as the hanging figure in the empty house or the Dark Man at the end of the Devil's Footsteps. But Jake seemed to have trapped himself into a corner, refusing to believe in this one thing, refusing to accept that the wolves of his nightmares could really come to life, and Bryan wasn't sure it was a good idea to break him out of it.

It had grown dark as they walked. *Dark? It's the middle of summer.* He tried to look at his watch, and couldn't even see the dial. It could have been no later than seven when they had left Stephen's house; night shouldn't fall for hours yet. And hadn't they been walking for a long time as they talked? Shouldn't they be at one of their houses by now? Where *were* they?

In the distance, a wolf howled.

~ XIII ~

JAKE'S EYES HAD SUDDENLY GONE WIDE, very white in the dimness. "Sounds like a . . . pretty big dog." He was walking a little faster. Bryan wasn't sure that was going to help.

"Er, Jake?" he asked softly. "Where do we turn here?"

The dark-haired boy came to a confused halt, as if he'd been walking on autopilot until then. He looked about them with increasing bewilderment. "I, er, well . . . what street are we on again?"

"I don't *know*," Bryan admitted, beginning to panic a little. How could they be lost? It was impossible.

"We must have—er, we must have taken a wrong turn somewhere. If we go back—"

"A wrong turn?" demanded Bryan. "Jake, we've lived here all our *lives*. It's not like this is a metropolis."

"Come on, Bryan, calm down." Oddly, it seemed as if Bryan

77

beginning to lose it was helping Jake regain his cool. "We're both spooked, and it all looks different in the dark. . . ."

"Dark? Jake, it's *July*."

"Then it must be . . . it must be a little bit later than we thought." He turned, ready to go back the way they'd come. "If we just—" He stopped dead.

Standing silently regarding them at the other end of the alley was a white wolf. Wolf? It was as big as a tiger. It regarded them through pale eyes devoid of expression. Somehow that was even worse than a glare of anger or hatred.

Its snow-colored coat seemed impossibly bright in the darkness, and Bryan's eyes threatened to water as he stared at it, not daring to move. He blinked, and in that fraction of an instant it was gone.

"Where did it go?" he demanded, shocked by the speed of it.

"I didn't see it move. . . ," said Jake. He sounded slightly faraway, not quite with it. His eyes were fixed on the spot where the wolf had just been standing.

Bryan looked around frantically, suddenly remembering the older boy's words from a few moments earlier. *You knew that as long as you could see them, you were safe, but once they disappeared . . .*

There was another wolf at the other end of the alley.

It looked just as blank-eyed and ghostly as the first. Bryan froze, forcing his eyes to stay open the way he did when he was waiting for his photo to be taken. The wolf didn't move like a real animal at all; it didn't yawn or sniff or twitch its ears. He couldn't even see it breathe.

There was a sound from behind him, and he whipped round. Nothing. He looked back, and the second wolf was

78

gone. He edged closer to Jake, who hadn't moved the whole time. "There must be two of them," he whispered.

"There'll be a whole pack," said Jake dully.

"We're gonna have to pick an end and run for it," Bryan said. There were no side shoots from this cramped, unfamiliar alley, and if the wolves moved in on them together . . .

"What for?" asked Jake in the same disconnected tone. "We can't outrun them."

"Well, we better do *something*!" snapped Bryan, a tide of panic once again rising. He couldn't watch both ends of the alley at once, and he was convinced that every time he looked away the wolves were returning to regard them with that same expressionless gaze. "Come on!"

Bryan decided that the end they'd been heading for was closest, and grabbed Jake by the arm to make him follow. The other boy stumbled after him willingly enough, but there was an odd blankness to his expression that Bryan really didn't like. He seemed like a rabbit caught in headlights, mentally and physically frozen.

They burst out of the end of the alley, Bryan's hands automatically tightening into fists—as if he could possibly hope to beat off such huge creatures with his bare hands.

No wolves.

"Where did they go?" He looked all around, saw nothing. It would have been better if he'd been able to see them.

They seemed to be at a nexus of narrow alleys—which was crazy, of course, because there was no place like that in Redford, nobody would build anything like this in any town. Narrow paths stretched off in at least eight directions, and the walls were high, far too high. He couldn't tell which alley they'd come from.

Was that a flicker of white at the end of one tunnel?

Tunnel? Weren't they alleyways a minute ago? The world was melting and reshaping itself, nightmare merging into reality as the Dark Man wrapped his grip around them. . . . Not just the wolves, but everything that came with them, visions harking back to primeval days of crouching in caves at the mercy of prowling beasts.

Suddenly, so vividly that for a second Bryan feared it was really happening, he had a mental image of eight wolves appearing, blocking the mouths of every possible exit and all converging on the center. . . .

"We've got to move!" He practically set his shoulder against Jake to shove the older boy into a randomly chosen tunnel. "Go! Go!"

This was it. They'd chosen, and if one of the wolves appeared in front of them . . . The walls and ceiling seemed to be closing in, and Bryan didn't think he had room to turn around even if he wanted to. Which was nuts, because Jake was ahead of him and still moving, and he was taller, broader in the shoulders. If he could still stumble onwards, Bryan had more than enough space. Except that he didn't.

He couldn't see anything past Jake, could only literally push him onwards, teeth gritted in anticipation. Anticipation of the moment when Jake stopped dead despite his pushing— or worse, when the wolf arrived from *his* end of the tunnel instead, and suddenly snapped at his heels . . .

So why *didn't* they? Where were they? Why were they waiting? He felt an insane urge to yell out to them to just go ahead and bite him, get it over with.

Of course, he knew the real reason why they hadn't come

for him and Jake yet. The monsters never just *attack*. First you have to have the stalking, and then the chase. . . .

Even as he thought that, an inrush of cool air struck his face as they stumbled out into the open. They had emerged from the mouth of a cave into a vast expanse of trees—

Oh God, the woods, please, not the woods—

But wait, these weren't Redford woods. They weren't any trees that had existed for these past few centuries, or maybe ever. They were fairy-tale trees—the kind of forest where lost children wandered helpless for days, where dark things could lurk for centuries undisturbed by humans.

"Where the hell are we?" he heard Jake mutter, but he couldn't have given an answer if he'd had breath to do it. It was insane, impossible that they should be here, and yet on some level it struck a chord so deep that it hardly even seemed unnatural. This wasn't a place, it was a nightmare—literally, the elements of every half-remembered fairy tale and fantasy story made solid. He almost expected to see Little Red Riding Hood come skipping through the trees . . . except, in this story, there would be no heroic woodcutters or happy endings.

In this story, the big bad wolves would close in, and tear you limb from limb.

There came another plaintive howl; in the distance, but closer than that other one had been, back in the alley. What had been the alley. Bryan glanced back towards the cave, but that was gone too, folded away like a prop that was no longer needed. When the Dark Man was in control, time and space were bent around to follow the rules of a nightmare . . . and the nightmare said that when the wolves came, you would be lost in the middle of the forest, with nowhere to run.

Another wolf voice joined the first, and another. He lost count as the lone howl swelled into a chorus, a sound that was at once terrifying and heartbreakingly mournful. The howls seemed to come from all around them, a veritable army of wolves somewhere in the distance.

They were surrounded.

~ XIV ~

THE WOLF CHORUS SUDDENLY CAME TO AN END, not in the gradual way it had started, but as abruptly as if a switch had been flipped. The sound hung in the silence for a long moment, and Bryan wasn't sure if it was a real echo, or just the memory of the howls reverberating inside his head.

Chilled to the bone by a sound that sent him right back to prehistory, Bryan instinctively reached out to snag Jake's arm—the only human contact in this desperately lonely place.

Bryan could feel the older boy trembling, and Jake flinched away at his touch. Bryan realized that however horrific this was for him, it must be so much worse for Jake—an enactment of the nightmare that had haunted him most of his life. Bryan had to look closely to even make out a decent guess at his expression.

"Jake, are you all right?" he said softly, although part of

him believed that however far away they were, the wolves would still hear everything. Their breathing, their heart-beats—probably even Jake's teeth chattering.

Jake certainly seemed to be shivering, with a violence that was quite frightening. "I'm so c-cold," he managed to force out.

Cold? Wasn't that supposed to be a symptom of being in shock? But what the hell *was* "shock," anyway? What were you supposed to do? Bryan didn't even have a coat or a sweater to offer him—he himself wore just a thin summer shirt, while Jake was still in his sports jacket.

Suddenly Bryan's memory shot him a flash of Jake digging in the pockets of that jacket. Trapped in the dimness of the house on King's Hill, rooting around for—

"Jake! Have you still got your lighter?"

"Huh?" Jake frowned, animation partially returning to his worryingly slack face, and then he started to fumble in his pockets. It seemed to take him forever to drag the cigarette lighter free, and his hands were shaking so badly he almost dropped it. Bryan snatched it from him quickly, scared that if it hit the ground they'd never find it.

It took him a moment to figure how to spark it off; though he wasn't shaking like Jake, his own fear numbed his fingers, and he'd never held a cigarette lighter before in any case. Finally he succeeded in producing a tiny flame. He realized he was probably destroying his night vision, and the lighter couldn't possibly provide any sort of meaningful warmth—and yet that single small point of heat and light seemed like the center of the universe.

It seemed to help steady Jake a little. "Where are they?" he asked nervously. His eyes were darting rapidly from place to place, but it was still a definite improvement over the non-responsive zombie, Bryan thought. It wasn't as if his fear was irrational, after all.

"I don't know," Bryan admitted, looking around himself. It was a fairly futile effort, night-blind as he was from staring at the flame of the lighter. But he couldn't leave any part of the forest unwatched for long without the hairs on his neck standing up as the certainty that a wolf was there, watching, crept over him.

"Why are we just *standing* here?" demanded Jake desperately.

"Where can we go?" Bryan asked rhetorically, but somehow the two of them started walking anyway. He didn't really believe that this forest could be anything less than endless, but even pretending to be doing something was better than just standing waiting for the pack to come and get them. There were wolves all around them, surely closing in.

Bryan felt that they ought to be running, but there was nowhere to run to, and when they couldn't see the wolves, nothing to run *from*. But this slow nervous progress was worse than headlong flight in a lot of ways. It felt less like an escape than like the quiet bit in a horror film just before the monster leaps out.

"I saw one!" hissed Jake, grabbing him tightly by the shoulder. Bryan followed his gaze, but there was nothing to see. With Jake's current state of mind, it was impossible to guess if he'd really seen anything or not.

Bryan came to an abrupt stop. "We're doing this wrong!" he said.

"What?" Jake demanded worriedly. He tugged at Bryan's arm. "Come on, keep moving!"

"No!" Something had clicked inside Bryan's brain, a memory of what they'd been talking over with Stephen earlier. "Don't you get it? We're going about this all wrong."

"Wrong? It's a nightmare! How can you do it wrong?" Jake exclaimed, voice rising with his panic.

"A nightmare—right!" Bryan clicked his fingers. "Fears, Jake! Like you were saying earlier. You can't get away from the fear by running."

"Easy for you to say! It's not your fear!"

Bryan gulped as a silver shadow flitted between two dark trees, not so far away. They had reached a sort of small clearing, more of a slightly larger gap between adjacent trees than anything else. "I think it's everybody's fear," he corrected. He turned and looked at the nearest tree. It was tall, thirty feet at the least, not gnarled and expansive like the trees in Redford woods but almost as straight as a telegraph pole.

Perhaps it was supposed to be impossible to climb—that seemed like a part of the nightmare, sure enough—but Bryan knew all about climbing trees. Adam had been a local champion at it, a school legend.

Adam. A chilling reminder, as if he needed it, that nightmare or not, there was no easy waking up from this. He went over to a tree and took hold of a branch.

"What are you doing?"

"Climbing. Help me," he grunted.

"You can't hide up there!" Jake cried, but he automatically stepped forward to give Bryan a boost.

"I'm not hiding." Bryan carefully handed the lighter across to him. "Don't drop it. It's our only chance."

"What chance?" Jake demanded. "It's only—"

"It's *fire*, Jake. Fire." He kept climbing. He didn't look

down now, not from fear of heights but because he could *feel* the wolves pressing in.

He grasped the nearest branch and yanked, and then lowered himself to the ground, almost falling in his haste. It broke off; the wood splintered easily. He snapped it in half, tossing one section quickly to Jake.

"What good is this supposed to do, Bryan?" Jake asked softly, not looking at him. Bryan followed his gaze to where pale eyes glinted at them in the moonlight.

In reply, Bryan simply lifted the lighter from Jake's unsteady hand, and brought the flame into contact with the end of the branch. It lit surprisingly easily, not at all like his experiences on long-ago bonfire nights. Maybe it was just the incredible dryness of the dead wood. Or maybe it was something else. . . .

He was turning to share the flame with Jake's length of wood, lit end tracing a path through the night like a child's sparkler, when something struck him in the back with the force of a runaway truck.

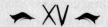

HIS FIRST CONFUSED THOUGHT WAS: *God, it's so heavy.* The wolves were as big as a full-grown man, maybe bigger, but you didn't expect something so ethereal to have such a weight to it.

Bryan would have hit the ground if he hadn't stumbled into Jake and sent them both staggering. The breath catapulted out of him with such force that he felt he was bringing his lungs up.

It was all confusion. How many wolves were in the clearing with them? Three? Four? Twenty? All of a sudden there seemed to be glinting fangs and flashing claws everywhere. Something ripped across his shin in a flash of pain that felt more intense than anything else he'd ever experienced, and he cried out.

He heard Jake yell across the clearing, but he couldn't tell if it was terror, pain, or an attempt at words. He could see the older boy flailing about blindly with the length of branch

Bryan had given him. Was he hitting anything? Bryan couldn't tell.

He was on the ground. How had he got there? Had he fallen? His injured leg had gone completely numb, as if it had been plunged into ice water.

There was a wolf leaning over him, right in his face. Its lips were drawn back over sharp fangs in a terrifying snarl, and yet it still managed to look somehow detached, uninvolved. Above it all.

Bryan lay looking up at it for a fraction of a second that lasted forever. He was paralyzed as much by the feeling that this was too surreal to be happening as by being winded. The wolves were still completely silent even in the attack; no growls, no snarls, not even the sound of their footfalls. He might have said they were ghosts if it hadn't been for the incredible weight of the wide paw bearing down on his chest.

Supernatural or not, the wolf was definitely solid. And now it was bending down towards him, seeming to move incredibly slowly, preparing to rip his throat out. And why stop it? Why not just lie here and be hypnotized by those terrible blank eyes, and wait for it to end . . . ?

Bryan wasn't even aware he was moving until it happened. His arm seemed to arc round of its own accord, bringing the burning branch he was somehow still holding solidly across the creature's snout.

It didn't even yelp or snarl aloud in protest. But he'd hurt it; he knew he had. The wolf melted back and the pressure on Bryan's chest abruptly eased. He pushed himself to his feet, still moving under the guidance of an automatic pilot he hadn't known he had.

He lashed out with the branch again, and the nearest

wolves fell back. How could it still be alight? It should have been extinguished when he fell, or even when he whipped it through the air. He had memories of bonfire nights, mock fighting with Adam with blazing sticks. Look away for a fraction of a second, and the flames were out. Yet this makeshift torch was burning as if it were a proper one, soaked in pitch or something like in the movies.

More unlikely still, the wolves seemed afraid of it. Never mind that they were huge, that there was a whole pack of them, that they were supernaturally quiet and strong and fast. They were genuinely afraid of him and his little burning stick.

I believe, he realized. The sudden thought almost struck him as funny, like listening to the hysterical fervor of a crowd caught up by an evangelist. But this wasn't an abstract, a concept to be swept up in and then come down from. This was deeper than that, going back to instincts that had been handed down and down for hundreds and thousands of years.

I believe in fire. That was what had been on his mind, hadn't it, when he climbed the tree in the first place?

The Dark Man took his power from what he found in your mind. But the shapes he borrowed from your nightmares came with rules attached. Garlic for vampires. Silver for werewolves. And a burning torch for animals with big teeth that came out of the darkness.

He knew that—of course he did, he'd seen the movies, read the stories, heard the same tales over and over and over again—but he hadn't realized how much he truly *believed* it until now. *Well, what do you know? I've got faith in something, after all.*

The wolves were still pulling back, melting away into the

trees. The attack; his automatic self-defense; the sudden epiphany—all of it had taken mere seconds. The wolves had come and gone in a flash. But a hell of a lot could happen in a flash.

"Jake?" He looked around, only now remembering he was not alone in this. As soon as the wolves had gone, the clearing had begun to lighten, as if dawn were coming in especially fast. Jake was on his back at the foot of a tree, unmoving, arms pulled up across his chest like an untidily arranged corpse.

"Jake?" He scrambled over to his friend, dropping his torch with barely a thought. The dying flicker of flame puffed into ashes.

He dropped to one knee beside the older boy, seeing the grimace of pain that contorted his features. "Jake, are you all right? Are you hurt?"

Jake opened his eyes, seemingly surprised to see him. "Bryan?" he said groggily.

Bryan looked down at himself, beginning to feel shaky now that the immediate danger had passed. "Yeah, it's me."

Jake pushed himself up awkwardly into a sitting position. "Where did they go?" he asked, glancing around. It was light again, the same summer evening they'd set out in. The trees looked different too; shorter, more familiar, more *alive*.

"They're gone," Bryan said. He tried a tentative grin. "I frightened them off." He could hardly believe that it had happened.

As if in response to the feeling of unreality, a sharp twinge of pain shot through his calf. He twisted round to look at the leg of his jeans: it had been shredded. "Oh, man, look at that!" He rolled the remains of his jeans up to get a look at the injury. It was shallow enough, three parallel scratches, but it was still bleeding, and it stung like crazy. "One of them got me," he grumbled.

"Me too," said Jake. He pulled his right hand away from where he'd been tightly gripping his left. It came away slick with bright red blood.

"Oh, Jesus!" Bryan rushed over to him, feeling his stomach lurch. He clamped Jake's hand back over the wound with his own. "Is it a bite?"

"I think so," said Jake. He still seemed faintly detached, though he wasn't the zombie he had been ten minutes—was that *all*?—earlier. He appeared more morbidly fascinated by the bite wound than troubled by it.

Bryan hurriedly ripped off his shirt and wrapped it as best he could across Jake's injury. "Keep that on it," he ordered, dragging Jake to his feet by his good arm.

"Where are we going?" asked Jake, staggering slightly.

"Hospital! Come on." Bryan picked a random direction and pushed through the trees.

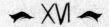

~ XVI ~

THEY EMERGED ALMOST IMMEDIATELY into the park. Bryan hadn't been there in five years, but still it all seemed heart-stoppingly familiar. The swings, the climbing frame with flaking paint, the burned-out shell of the games hut ... and behind him the woods. Suddenly the sense of his brother's presence was everywhere, choking him, more powerful than he'd felt it anywhere except perhaps in Adam's own room.

He might have frozen up, if it hadn't been for the desperate urgency of getting Jake some medical attention. Even so, he stumbled through the long grass as if he were drunk, trying not to see anything that would spark off those memories, memories that were too painful to see and too precious to give up.

It didn't work. Everything—the scent of the grass, the feel of the setting sun on his bare shoulders—was as powerful as a photograph, triggering off random fragments of recollection.

His head was filled with laughter, Adam's boyish laugh seeming so creepy when it only echoed inside his head. Adam laughing, Adam running, Adam saying, "Let's go into the woods."

Come on, it'll be so cool. What are you afraid of, Bryan? Mum and Dad won't even know. We can sneak in and be back before they come and get us. What are you afraid of?

Well, if Adam had been here today, he could've told him. *Yes, I was afraid. I was the little kid scared of monsters, and you were the tough guy who didn't believe in them. And who was right, Adam? Who was right, all along? Because the monsters are real. The monsters are real, and they can really hurt you.*

He stumbled through the streets with Jake in tow, locked in an internal dialogue with his long-vanished brother. The ghosts of memory had become so powerful he was barely aware of the rest of the world, could easily have stepped out in front of a truck and not noticed when it hit him.

But there were no trucks. No concerned little old ladies peered over their hedges at these two battered and bleeding teenage boys. Nobody asked, "Hey, are you kids all right?" But that was part of Redford too. Part of the not-seeing.

Bryan came back to himself somewhere in the hospital car park. Perhaps Jake had known where they were going, or perhaps his own body had been under the control of that same autopilot he'd only just discovered he had. He couldn't remember anything of the journey.

He had a suspicion there were tears on his face, though he couldn't remember shedding them. Well, it wasn't as if they would look out of place under the circumstances.

They rushed into the emergency room and Bryan called desperately for attention. He said something about a big dog that had attacked them, barely listening to his own cover story as he told it. But nobody else seemed to be listening to it either; the doctors took them both in calmly and competently, the other patients glanced at them with little curiosity. Bryan wondered how many times these people dealt with wolf bites, piranha bites, vampire bites; a thousand impossible injuries masterminded by the Dark Man. And none of it would be remarked upon, any more than people seemed to notice how often kids went missing or anything else that happened in Redford.

He lost sight of Jake as he was taken to have his scratches cleaned by a nurse. They wanted to give him some kind of shot—tetanus, he supposed—but for that they needed his parents' permission.

The desk contacted his father; his mother would no doubt have taken to her bed by this stage in the evening. These days she seemed to need at least sixteen hours of sleep at a time, as if she could somehow hide from the world by getting back in bed and switching the lights off.

"Your father'll be here to pick you up fairly soon," the nurse told him.

Bryan was almost surprised. "Did he sound . . . worried?" he asked gingerly, feeling an odd twinge almost like excitement in his stomach. He felt almost light-headed at the idea that maybe his getting hurt had cut through the layers of insulation that existed between him and his parents.

"Jenny explained that it's barely a scratch," the nurse reassured him, completely failing to pick up the point of the inquiry . . . but then, what normal person would? "She said he sounded pretty calm."

Bryan suspected that this Jenny person who'd actually spoken to his dad might have had a better idea of what he was talking about. "Calm" was more of a euphemism than a description; "zombie-like," "disconnected," "detached" might be better words.

So much for hoping that a little minor physical damage might provoke a reaction. Bryan resisted a sudden powerful impulse to leap up and start smashing things. He could see a few things around that would make truly satisfying crashes. . . .

What does it take to get through to these people?

The nurses were busy, and once he was cleaned and jabbed, he was kicked back out into the waiting room. Jake joined him a few minutes later, sporting bandages across the lower half of his palm.

"I look like I've been at war," he said, shaking his head, as he collapsed into the plastic chair beside Bryan. He held up his hands and grimaced at them; the minor burn he'd received that morning was beginning to look very red. He sighed. "What next?"

"Oh, we're not done yet," Bryan prophesied darkly. Earlier, the idea of fighting the Dark Man had been a pipe dream, a way of making themselves feel as if they were actually doing something. But now their enemy was bringing the war to them, and he wasn't sure they'd be safe anywhere anymore.

Jake sighed again, and ran the unbandaged hand through his spiky hair. "Still . . . you scared them off."

Bryan couldn't help letting a grin spread across his features. "Yeah. I did that. Thanks to your cigarette lighter."

In truth, he realized, he hadn't so much scared the wolves as . . . neutralized them. The Dark Man had wrapped Jake's nightmare around them, but Bryan had changed the course of it. The Dark Man's power came from making you believe he could hurt you . . . but the other things you believed had power too. There *was* a way to fight back.

Of course, a painful twinge from his clawed leg reminded him, there was a big difference between being able to temporarily deflect the Dark Man's attack and being safe from him.

"Oh, hell!" Jake suddenly jerked upright. "I think I told that nurse we used a cigarette lighter to scare it off. What if she told my dad? He doesn't know I smoke."

"Oh, just tell him it was mine," Bryan said, shrugging.

"Won't your parents be mad, then? Mine would go nuts— at least I'm *nearly* old enough."

Yeah, right. "No. They won't care."

The outside door suddenly swung open, and a worried-looking middle-aged couple burst through it. The short, dark-skinned man and his elegant little wife should have looked totally at odds with their tall, athletically built son, and yet Bryan could see Jake in them.

He could also see their concern, obvious in the way they fluttered about like trapped birds; asking Jake questions, asking the nurses questions, clucking over the bandage in disbelief. Jake himself looked awkward and embarrassed.

When they'd spent time ascertaining whether he was really all right, that his hand wasn't going to get infected, that it wasn't going to swell up and drop off, their attention turned to Bryan.

"This is my friend Bryan Holden," Jake explained. And then they fussed over *him*, looking at his scratches and exclaiming in dismay. Bryan felt stifled by the attention, although not in a way Jake would have understood.

Stop it, just stop it, okay? You're not my parents, why are you doing this? Why are you fussing over some kid who's not even your own? Just stop it.

"Where are your parents, Bryan?" asked Mr. Steinbeck worriedly.

What's it to you? "Er . . . my dad's on his way here," he explained, glad that for once it didn't have to be a lie.

"We'll wait with you," Jake's mother said kindly.

What? No! No, bad idea. "Um, really, I'm okay. You don't have to do that."

"Oh, we insist," said Mr. Steinbeck magnanimously. "Least we can do. Our Jake's lucky he had you with him."

So he was forced to sit there, swinging his legs in that uncomfortable plastic chair and sending out psychic messages to the Steinbecks that they had to go home, they'd left the oven on, they'd forgotten to lock the door in their hurry, their favorite TV program was about to start—anything at all to get them out of there before his dad arrived.

It didn't work.

⌐ XVII ⌐

THE FAMILIAR, HALF-STOOPED FIGURE of Bryan's father shuffled into the room. He was barely forty, still sandy-haired and with no sign of a middle-aged paunch, and yet he looked very old. Mr. Steinbeck was short, but Alan Holden looked *small*—as if whatever it was that made him an adult, a grown-up, a father, had been drained out of him.

No high-speed dash or shouted questions here. He just looked about the waiting room blearily, as if he'd already forgotten why he was supposed to be there and whether it was important. Bryan got up from the chair and ran towards him.

"Dad, I'm over here." As if his father simply hadn't seen, instead of being totally unseeing.

"Oh, hello, son." A soft smile that didn't touch the sad gray eyes.

Bryan babbled on, answering all the questions the Steinbecks had asked so that nobody would get to notice how his father didn't ask them. "Look, I got these scratches on the back of my leg—they're not so bad, though. The nurses cleaned them up for me. There was this big dog that attacked us, that's me and Jake—that's him over there." He pointed.

His father inspected the scratches solemnly, and nodded. He offered the Steinbecks a brief smile that wasn't any more genuine than the one he'd given his son.

Perhaps sensing the awkwardness about to descend, Jake's father hopped down from his chair and glided over to pump hands. "Eli Steinbeck," he said, and nodded to his elegantly presented other half. "My wife, Adira."

Something like animation returned to Bryan's father as he shook hands. This was familiar, formal, the act he put on as a matter of course when he went out into the workplace every day. "Alan Holden. Ellen's still back at the house, guarding the dinner—she was afraid the place would burn down if she went out." A brief flicker of fake amusement.

Bryan knew that was a lie; his mother wouldn't be cooking, wouldn't be doing anything. She just wouldn't have come out because she hardly ever left the safe cocoon of her bed anymore. He also knew that even though it was a lie, even though his father must know that Bryan knew that, neither of them would say anything about it.

Dull silence had descended again, and as usual Bryan took charge, filling the gaps, smoothing it over. *Nothing to see here, everything's fine. A little bit of awkwardness? Surely you imagined it. Everything's nice and normal here.* "Um, we should be getting back. Mum'll be worried." Huh. That was a laugh and a half, wasn't it?

"Yes, yes." Another horrible moment of blankness before

his father seemed to click to the meaning of the words. "Yes," he said again, more strongly. "Come on, Bryan. I've got the car outside."

As he left, Bryan's eyes met Jake's. For a second he caught a flash of sympathy and understanding, and then he was walking out of there, following his father to the car for a silent ride back to their dead home. As he slid into the front seat and belted himself in, it was as if he could hear the conversation going on back inside the hospital behind them.

Oh, what a strange little man. . . .

Now, now, dear, perhaps he's just a little distracted. . . .

Holden . . . wasn't that the little boy who disappeared a few years back? Aaron, Adam, something like that?

Hmm, yes. Yes, now that you mention it. That must have been the father.

Poor man. Probably hasn't been the same since.

And, worst of all: *Oh, that poor boy.* The weight of other people's sympathy, even imagined, was something Bryan didn't think he could bear.

He and his father didn't talk on the ride home, but that was far from unusual. The car radio was never on, except when Bryan asked for it. He usually only did that when he was out with both his parents, and the silence between the three of them became too oppressive. Then he would tune into the first news station he could find, preferring the sound of voices, any voices, to some inane pop song that would only make the silence worse.

Tonight, for the first time, he barely noticed it. He was hardly aware of the journey at all, mind churning the day's events over and over.

It was late when they got back; time seemed to have twisted up and lengthened, and rather than try to watch TV he just took a shower and slipped into his pajamas. He inspected the scratches in the mirror on the way; though there was no more blood, they sketched livid lines against his pale skin. It was ridiculous that anyone could have accepted their story of a wild dog; it was easy to see that an animal the size of a tiger must have made these marks.

But as he crawled between the sheets in the stifling heat of the July night, Bryan's mind was not on his injuries. All he could think of was their victory; minor, perhaps more technical than anything else, but the fact remained—for once, the Dark Man hadn't won.

He didn't beat us. This time, we didn't just escape—we turned him aside. We didn't let him beat us. So maybe, maybe, there was some sort of hope after all.

His newfound confidence didn't follow him into his dreams.

He was running, running, stumbling through the forest. *No, that's not right. We didn't run away . . . where's Jake?*

Bryan was alone, alone in the darkness apart from the wolf pack at his heels. *Can't fight it. Not on my own.* All he could do was keep running.

Except that he was going deeper and deeper inside, towards the heart of the woods. *No! Feet, where are you taking me? Not in here!* But he couldn't turn aside, couldn't even look back over his shoulder. And he didn't want to; he knew without seeing that the wolves had changed, grown huge, become dark, malevolent things. No longer solemn and majestic ghosts, sadly undertaking something unavoidable, but now obscenely gleeful, glorying in the chase and its inevitable conclusion.

And it was, of course, inevitable.

The clearing. A clearing that would never appear on any map of the Redford woods no matter how many times the surveyors walked it. A clearing that never could be mapped, because whichever direction you chose when you started walking—or better still, running—it would always be there.

And the stones. Thirteen stones that he couldn't turn away from. Even now, heedless of the wolf-things behind him, Bryan found himself slowing, coming to a stop. He stopped before the first of the steps, and thought, *This time, this time, I'm gonna be able to walk away.*

But even as he was thinking of escape, his feet betrayed him.

One in fire, two in blood, three in storm, four in flood.

He had been crazy, thinking for even a moment that his "victory" against the wolves had meant anything. You could deflect the Dark Man, perhaps, but really that wasn't anything but another way of running away from him.

Five in anger, six in hate, seven fear, evil eight.

You could run away, and run away, and run away . . . but you couldn't do it forever. Every time, it was a little bit closer, a little bit of a tighter scrape. He wasn't getting away because he was clever, because he was strong, because he was brave. . . . It was luck. Nothing more than luck.

Nine in sorrow, ten in pain, eleven death, twelve life again.

Or was it even that? Was he deluding himself that these escapes even meant anything? The Dark Man was just playing with him, like a cat. Taking dark amusement in his prey's continual optimism, the way the mouse kept thinking that this time, *this time,* maybe the paws wouldn't come sweeping down to knock him back to where he started.

But sooner or later, the Dark Man would tire of playing. And it would come down to this. The same thing it always came down to.

Thirteen steps to the Dark Man's door. Won't be turning back no more.

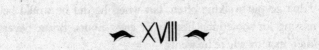

~ XVIII ~

IT WAS A BRIGHT SUNDAY MORNING, already warm when he woke, but Bryan was chilled by the sweat that had descended on him in the night. He dressed quickly, cursing as he got a good look at the condition of the clothes slung over the back of his bedroom chair. His best jeans were shredded, and his shirt from the night before was a rag, and caked with Jake's dried blood. He quickly balled it up and threw it in the bin with a grimace of distaste.

It wasn't just his clothes bearing the marks of the past night's struggle. The long scratches across his calf that had barely bothered him the night before were lines of red-hot fire, now that the adrenaline had faded. He descended the stairs at an awkward hop, nearly falling on his face as he came to the bottom. There were fourteen steps in his own home, and he always jumped down to the hall floor from the eleventh—that way there were really only a dozen stairs. It was a completely automatic habit, but with his injured leg he misjudged, and made it into the living room limping badly.

His father was already awake, of course, feet up in front of the TV. What his mother had gained in sleeping time his father had lost; Bryan often heard him roaming the house in the early hours of the morning, and sometimes the front door would slam late at night when he went out for a walk. He didn't go out walking often, but when he did he would be missing for something like six or eight hours. Bryan never knew exactly where he went.

The walks were his way of letting off steam, while his wife took to her bed. They felt the bad atmosphere inside the house, the buildup of pressure, as much as Bryan did. But though he was the kid and they were supposedly the grownups, they never dealt with it any better than he did. They just had different means of running away.

Because all three of them needed to get away from *this*; every morning, every evening, that same game of Let's Pretend.

Bryan couldn't care less if he never got a hug or some dramatic declaration of love. He would have liked to argue about whether he'd done his homework, or be warned not to steal the chocolate brownies. Sunday had been his mother's day for an early-morning baking spree, and he and Adam would sneak in and grab whatever was cooling—always getting caught and scolded, but never before they'd managed to snatch at least one prize. He remembered the week his mother had decided to bake bread instead, and how she'd thrown her head back and laughed at their indignant expressions.

He hadn't heard that laugh for five years. His mother hadn't stopped laughing, but now it was always her polite laugh, the one she'd used to use when his father's boss made

106

some kind of stupid joke that wasn't really funny. Bryan thought listening to that laugh was even worse than hearing her cry.

His father had always been quiet, but once it had been a warm silence, and now it was cold. Bryan thought briefly of the great aura of comforting warmth that had flowed from Stephen's dad yesterday, and hated himself for it.

He sat down on the settee beside his father, and tried to watch the TV with him. It was some kind of film, but it might just as easily have been cartoons or the news. The TV was always on, but nobody really watched it.

Nevertheless, he tried. "Morning, Dad. What're you watching?"

"Some old war movie," mumbled his father, with a shrug. Despite his lack of interest, his eyes were fixed on the screen.

"Who's in it?" Bryan asked. He hated his own voice too, the way it somehow managed to come out bright and brittle just like theirs when he tried to talk to them. It didn't sound that way when he was talking to Stephen and Jake.

His father shrugged again. "You know. That guy. With the ears and the flat hair." Once that would have been an invitation to make fun of such a pathetic description, but now it just didn't seem worth the effort. He wouldn't get a response anyway.

Bryan was gripped by a sudden urge to pipe up, the way he had when he was nine or ten: *Come on, Dad, let's go to the cinema. Let's go down to the river and make paper boats. Let's go wake Mum up and we can all drive down to the beach for the day. Let's go—*

Let's go down to the woods.

The urge abruptly passed, and Bryan got up and made

himself breakfast instead. Anyway, all his father would have said was "Maybe next week, Bryan," or "I'm sure you'd much rather be out with your friends instead of us old fogies."

Bryan wondered if either of his parents knew that until about three days before, he hadn't had any friends.

Were Jake and Stephen his friends? He supposed they were. Maybe they'd only been thrown together because of their shared fear of the Dark Man—but hey, weren't you supposed to make friends with people you had something in common with?

Despite everything, he was feeling oddly energized, better than he had for a long time. Being under constant attack by the Dark Man in all his guises paled in comparison to the relief of actually having someone to *talk* to.

Bryan polished off his cereal and threw the bowl down in the sink. "Dad, I'm going out with my friends."

He limped over to Stephen's house first. His leg was really beginning to hurt now; he hoped he wouldn't have to do any more running. *No. No running,* he thought, remembering his nightmare from the night before. Running just wasn't good enough anymore.

Stephen was, as he'd suspected, already up and dressed. He answered the door, and his little sister yelped in dismay as he gave the whole street a view of her Barbie pajamas. "*Stephen!*" she cried, thumping his shoulders. He just laughed, and Bryan thought of how Adam had always done stuff like that to him.

"Oh, I don't know what she's yowling about," said Stephen, hopping down from the front doorstep and shaking his head. "It's eight o'clock on a Sunday morning—who's watching? Who would want to?"

"Did you ask her about Marcie whatshername and the ghosts in the woods?" Bryan asked as Stephen closed the door behind him. Stephen shrugged.

"She just thinks I'm making fun of her now. Keeps going on about how there really *are* ghosts, and it's not her fault I'm too dumb to believe it. And I can't exactly say, 'Yeah, I know there are, you don't need to try and prove it to me,' you know?"

"Yeah." He remembered the days after Adam had first disappeared, telling his story to an endless chain of people; the worst had been the ones who'd *acted* as if they believed him. Talking over his story with him in condescending voices, and all the time constantly digging for what they thought must be the real truth. No wonder the darkness in Redford had been buried for so long, when even those who believed in it didn't know who they could trust to listen to them.

They started walking, taking off for Jake's house without even discussing it, and Stephen noticed Bryan's limp. "Hey, what happened to your leg, man?"

Bryan pulled up the leg of his jeans to reveal the red lines of the scratches, and Stephen sucked in a shocked breath. "Wolves," Bryan said shortly.

"Wolves?" Not surprisingly, it didn't take Stephen too long to click to what had happened. "Where?"

"In the forest."

"*What* forest?" Stephen demanded incredulously.

"Exactly," said Bryan, raising his eyebrows pointedly.

"What about Jake? Is he okay?" asked Stephen worriedly.

"He got bitten, but he's all right," Bryan explained. "He was pretty shook up, though—he's got some kind of wolf phobia."

"I'm not surprised." Stephen seemed genuinely shocked, as if until then he hadn't truly believed that any of them might actually get seriously hurt. "They got close enough to *bite* you? How did you get away?"

"I chased them off!" Bryan told him excitedly. "I had Jake's lighter, and I got this bit of wood, right, and it just lit up into a torch and—" He broke off, shaking his head. "It was incredible, man, you should've seen it!" He could still barely believe it had happened himself.

"Whoa." Stephen was silent for a moment, and then he started to smile. "It *worked*, then. Standing up to him."

"It really worked, yeah!" Bryan agreed. Then he sobered a little. "But it's not enough. Sure, we defended ourselves, but that's not much better than running, when you think about it."

"So what should we do? Try to . . . attack?" Stephen asked hesitantly.

"How can we do that?" Bryan demanded, feeling the moment of optimism begin to peel away. "You might fight *one* nightmare, but the Dark Man is bigger than that. He's the source of it all. How can you fight that?"

"I don't know." Stephen looked at the ground, scuffing his sneakers against the gravel path. "We need to know why this is happening, Bryan. Why here? How did it ever end up like this? Maybe—" He shrugged. "Maybe if we knew *that*, we could . . ." He let his voice trail off.

Bryan rubbed his face uneasily. "I don't know. We'll get Jake, and then we'll think about it. Because we're gonna have to. We can't stay lucky forever."

That much, he was certain of.

~ XIX ~

THEY MET UP WITH JAKE, and Stephen exclaimed over the condition of his hand. Jake's parents were already up, working in the garden. They seemed a little reluctant to let him go out, but finally they gave in.

"Nice to see you making some new friends," his father commented. Jake reacted to that with something like a disguised flinch, and Bryan knew he was thinking of Lucy. He suspected that Jake had probably spent the past year in the kind of self-enforced loneliness he himself was very familiar with, throwing himself into his research project. Jake's connection with Bryan and Stephen was really more of the same, but the Steinbecks didn't know that. They probably looked at their son and were glad he was at last moving on.

Of course, Bryan's own parents couldn't have noticed even if he was—because *they* weren't.

Bryan supposed that actually, he and Jake *were* moving

on; just not in the right direction. They weren't turning away from what had happened—they were heading right into the center of it. It wasn't enough to come to terms with it, when you knew it was still happening to other people's friends and brothers all around you.

How long? he thought. *How long until the next kid goes missing?*

Maybe Jake had been having similar thoughts, for as soon as he was out of earshot of his parents, he asked, "What's our next move?"

"The train station?" Stephen said hesitantly. He seemed less decisive than he had before, perhaps shaken by the extent of the others' injuries.

"Yeah." Bryan breathed out slowly. "Yeah, I think we have to."

The scratches on his leg stung as they walked, the rough material of his jeans rubbing painfully against the wounds. It was just a fraction too hot to be comfortable, and his clothes stuck to his skin. He didn't feel much like any kind of adventuring hero.

He wasn't a hero. He was just *tired.* Tired of all these years lived in the Dark Man's shadow, waiting for the jaws of the trap to close. Better to do something, anything, even if it was futile.

They trailed through the town, nobody marking their passage, nobody caring if they'd seen. Just three boys, out looking for trouble, no doubt. Out for a bit of fun.

Yeah, it's all fun and games, all right. Bryan thought back to an old playground game from a lifetime ago. *What's the time, Mr. Wolf?* You got to creep up on the big bad wolf, but if he saw you coming, then it was the end of the road for you. And if you managed to sneak up and grab him, then *you* got to be the wolf—but was that really winning, when you got right down to it? You could eat, or be eaten, but you couldn't say, "Hey, let's stop, I don't want to do this anymore." There was no room to opt out and say you weren't playing.

They made their way down the steps to the station. There were people coming and going even on a Sunday, but nobody walked around behind the shops to the forgotten square of weeds and broken bricks. Of course, why would they have reason to? It was the kind of place nobody would go.

Nobody but kids. Woods and haunted houses and overgrown patches where nothing got built . . . They were all *children's* places. Adults would pass them by without a thought or a backward glance, but for children they had a powerful pull of fascination.

They stood for a moment outside the station building, and exchanged glances. Jake shrugged slightly, and Stephen let his breath out slowly. They both looked at Bryan, as if he should somehow be the leader.

He wanted to angrily reject the position, but instead he just sighed. "Okay, then," he said quietly. He led the way around the corner to face—

Absolutely nothing. He was looking at a wide expanse of undeveloped space, with nothing but dirt piles, long grass, and old bricks. Several rusting lengths of pipe lay half buried in the ground a few yards away, as if they'd been put there for some building project, and then just forgotten.

They all looked around, bunched together for protection as if subconsciously waiting for something to leap out at them. Nothing moved.

"Bricks," Jake observed dryly, after a moment.

"*Old* bricks." Bryan nudged one with a foot, and some of the ancient mortar still clinging to it crumbled away. It was slightly blackened, as if it had been through a fire, although he somehow doubted anybody had been using these bricks for a barbecue pit.

"There's nothing here," said Stephen, almost wonderingly. He edged closer to Bryan, as if this realization were even more unnerving than finding the worst of the Dark Man's arsenal pointed at them.

"Are you sure this is really, well . . . one of his places?" Jake asked after a moment. "I mean, couldn't it just have been—?"

Bryan shook his head slowly. No. It was too still, too quiet, too . . . removed. As if the station were not just steps away, but a million miles away. And—"If this was just a normal place . . . why aren't there fifteen houses and a supermarket up here? It looks like this place has been left empty forever."

"But why?" Jake said slowly. "What was here?" He wandered through the long grass, stepping over piles of abandoned bricks.

"You're the history expert," Bryan reminded him. He just shrugged.

"Maybe it's because it's Sunday?" Stephen volunteered hesitantly, still looking around uneasily for evidence of the Dark Man. "It *is* supposed to be a holy day."

"Not my holy day, I'm Jewish," Jake objected. "And that really didn't help me much yesterday." He flexed his bandaged hand to make his point.

"Religion won't help," Bryan told them. "Not us, anyway. I'm fifteen years old! It's way easier for me to believe in monsters than in religion." *Especially after what happened five years ago.*

"This could have been where the old mill used to be, maybe," Jake suggested, glancing back over his shoulder as he walked. "Except I think that was further south. I'm trying to remember what it was that they knocked down when they—ow!" He stumbled in the long grass and almost lost his footing, narrowly avoiding falling flat on his face.

"More bricks?" Bryan guessed, but Jake frowned, and knelt down.

"I don't think so . . . ," he said slowly. He looked up at them, dark eyes startled. "Come and see this!"

The other two scrambled over anxiously. "What is it?" Bryan asked them.

"Oh, it's just a piece of wooden board stuck in the ground," Stephen observed, straightening up. Jake shook his head.

"Nope. Listen." He rapped the board with his knuckles, and there was a hollow sound, as if there was space beneath. He stood up, and stamped suddenly towards the center of it. In a crunch of splintering wood, his foot went straight through.

"Careful!" Bryan snapped urgently, grabbing him by the shoulder.

"Whoa." Jake looked sheepish as he stepped back. "Little bit more rotten than I thought, maybe."

Stephen lay down on his belly to peer through the gap. "What's down there?"

"Can you see anything?" Bryan asked, hovering by his shoulder.

Stephen gave him a look. "Yeah, fortunately, when they built the place they used extra-long-life lightbulbs."

"Only asking," Bryan said, shrugging defensively. He turned to the older boy. "Jake, what do you think it is?"

"Cellar of some kind, I would imagine," Jake said, with an intrigued look. "It must have belonged to one of the buildings that was here before."

Stephen pushed himself up with a frown. "How come it's still here? I mean, you don't just leave some rotten old cellar hatch where anybody can fall down it."

"In Redford, maybe you do," Bryan reminded him softly.

He knew instinctively that this wasn't just some random oversight, an empty cellar boarded up and forgotten. There was a reason why this place had long stood abandoned. There was probably a reason why the three of them had stumbled over it here, now, when they were looking for the root of the Dark Man's power here.

Echoing his thoughts, Stephen said grimly, "I don't think we want to go down there."

Bryan straightened up. It seemed to him that although it was just as sunny as it had been a moment before, something had shifted, and suddenly there was no more warmth in the day. "No. But I don't think we have a choice."

THEY BROKE AWAY THE REST of the rotting wood by hand. It was horribly slick and slimy to the touch, and Bryan couldn't tell if it had been stained black originally, or some foul mold had got into it. The top rungs of a ladder were still hanging underneath, but none of the boys risked trusting them.

"Better off jumping," Stephen observed. With more overhead light spilling in, they could see it wasn't that long a drop.

Not long—but Bryan remembered just about the time he struck the bottom that he'd hurt his leg. He staggered as he landed, and swore. Jake's worried face appeared up above. "Hey, are you all right down there?"

"Yeah, I just forgot . . . my brain," he finished vaguely, as he looked around.

The space was disappointingly small. It was little more than a brick-walled cube, narrow enough in both directions that if he stretched out his arms he could touch two walls at once. The floor was loosely packed earth, and the walls bulged inwards slightly, making it even more claustrophobic. There was a stale, choking smell of mud and decay.

"There's nothing down here," he announced, tilting his head back to look up at the others. He had to squint against the sunshine that spilled down into his face.

He looked at the broken old ladder on the wall. Only five rungs remained, and those looked rotten through and splintered, but it was easy enough to judge the space and count how many steps there must once have been.

Eleven . . . twelve . . . thirteen.

Thirteen steps to the Dark Man's door . . .

"Wait, what's that?" Stephen's voice echoed oddly in the enclosed space.

"What's what?" Bryan asked.

"In the corner. Just a little—"

"I don't see it," he said, frowning.

"Move over, Jake." A moment later, Stephen dropped down into the hole, managing a much more elegant landing than Bryan's. With the two of them down there, rubbing shoulders, it was stiflingly cramped. "Look, there."

Stephen must have had sharp eyesight to have spotted it from up above, for what he picked up from the ground seemed like nothing more than a small scrap of dark leather, crushed into a flattened shape. It lay in Stephen's palm for a moment as they puzzled over it.

"It's a shoe," Bryan finally said, recognizing it despite its tiny size.

"It's a doll's shoe," Stephen supplied, and he could have smacked his forehead. That made a lot more sense. . . . Or didn't.

"Why would a doll have been down here?" The room

seemed nonsensically small for a storage cellar, and besides, something like a doll would surely have been ruined in a few days down in the dirt and damp.

"Where there's a doll, there's usually a little girl attached," Stephen, familiar with little sisters, pointed out.

That thought was even more disquieting. "What would a little girl be doing down here?" Bryan looked up at the small square of sunlight, and Jake's anxious face. It was smaller than a prison cell down here, and the way out would have seemed impossibly high to a child.

The mental image of pale-faced, frightened children shut away down in the dark was so vivid that, for a moment, Bryan could almost feel them pressed in around him and Stephen. He imagined their voices: hushed whispers, plaintive cries, muffled and echoing and distorted by the bricks and packed-earth walls. The overwhelming babble of a crowd . . . yet at the same time, a sound of unbearable loneliness.

Bryan realized, with a jolt of shock, that he knew that voice. How could he not? He heard it in his dreams; he'd been hearing it sing to him for the past five years.

One in fire, two in blood, three in storm and four in flood . . .

Suddenly the floor lurched beneath him. "What the— Jesus!" He scrambled backwards.

"What's happening?" Jake called down urgently. The ground was buckling beneath Bryan's feet, as if something was wriggling beneath it, fighting to get out.

"Bryan, look out!" Stephen shouldered him urgently aside as something pale and snakelike burst through the brickwork directly in front of them. It looked like nothing so much as the blind, questing head of a giant worm, and they flinched away in revulsion.

More were breaking through the walls all around them, shunting aside bricks with violent force. "What *are* they?" Bryan demanded, grabbing Stephen by the shoulder.

"Roots!" The moment Stephen said so it seemed to crystallize into truth, the nightmare of walls eaten away until they collapsed made high-speed reality.

Stephen threw his head back to look up. "We have to get out of here before the whole place comes down."

Dark earth was spilling in through the gaps in the brickwork, pouring as easily and quickly as piled sand. One of the probing roots prodded Bryan's shoulder, and he slapped it away with a cry.

"Bryan, take my hand!" That was Jake, up above, but he already seemed further away. They were no longer in a tight little box of a room, but at the bottom of a deep pit like a well shaft, and the walls were crumbling. . . .

I know it's not real. I know it's not like that, I know it's not real—Bryan knew it, but the knowledge had no power, no force of belief to drive it. He knew, but it was getting choked to death by the fear of suffocation, trapped under here, drowning with lungs full of dirt. . . .

Stephen, already climbing up, grabbed him by the wrist, and tried to haul him upwards. "Come on, Bryan! You gotta climb!"

And suddenly Bryan was half plunged into the past, remembering his brother's impatient snarls and muffled curses when Bryan froze partway through some tricky venture. Adam was the climber, the one who always went scrambling in and out of danger with athletic ease, while Bryan was forced to tag along behind him, smaller, slower, not so brave. . . .

Adam should be the one who'd survived, not him. Adam

was always better at everything. What cruel trick of fate could ever have stolen him away and left his worthless younger brother behind?

"Come *on!*" Stephen tugged on the loose cloth of his shirt and Bryan struggled to follow him, scrabbling for a foothold on bricks that were suddenly slick and glassily smooth. *You climbed a tree with no branches in the dark, what's a brick wall full of holes supposed to be to you?* But the calm confidence that had settled over him the night before had melted into nothingness.

He tried to climb, but roots were bursting through the walls all around him, shattering bricks and sending dark earth pouring down to pelt him. His injured leg burned as if it were on fire. Bryan spat fragments of dirt, and tried to blank out the pressing image of being buried alive in a cascade of bricks as the walls came down.

Beside him Stephen cried out, and Bryan couldn't see why but he grabbed him by the arm anyway, and tried to haul him up. How had he got ahead of Stephen, anyway? And why did the dim light of freedom high above seem even further away?

Something snagged Bryan's ankle. He yelped and kicked out, trying to break free, but the tendril wrapped around his leg was as thick and strong as a tree root. It tugged at him determinedly, seeking to dash him against the walls of the shaft and let him fall to his doom.

With a surge of desperation he slammed his trapped leg against the bricks, hard, and felt the grip momentarily loosen. He tore himself away, feeling as if his ankle were being pulled out of its socket, and hauled himself a few feet further up. Both of his legs burned now, and his left arm was locked through Stephen's, trying not to lose him as they climbed together. The other boy seemed to be struggling, panicked by the narrowness of the shaft and the desperate ascent.

A few feet further up he should emerge onto the grass above. There was no more a brick shaft going down into the depths of the earth here than there was a fairy-tale forest in the middle of Redford. He *knew* that.

He knew that. But he had to believe it.

As more dirt and brick dust rained down on him, Bryan squeezed his eyes shut and climbed blindly. He tried to force the image of the cellar as he'd first seen it into his mind, and remember it. A tiny brick-lined chamber, he'd *thought* how small it was. He'd jumped in—if it hadn't been for his battered leg, he wouldn't have noticed the drop at all. And yet he was still climbing, pulling himself up hand over hand over hand . . .

It's only a couple of feet. You know it's only a couple of feet.

Something thudded painfully into the small of his back and he almost lost his grip, but he still didn't open his eyes. Instead he struggled to fix the memory image in his mind, tried to make it more real than the chokingly persistent terror of the illusion. All his senses were telling him he was about to be hauled down into the depths of the earth and die, but he forced the messages down, tried to drive them away. With a desperate heave of his muscles, he reached up—

—And grabbed Jake's hand.

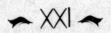

~ XXI ~

BRYAN SCRAMBLED UP INTO THE SUNSHINE, panting. The splintered remains of the wooden hatch jabbed him in the stomach, but he didn't care. Together he and Jake hauled up Stephen, who coughed and clutched his chest as if he'd been breathing dirt.

Bryan glanced back down the hole he'd just crawled out of. For a moment it seemed that as he looked down he was gazing into the depths of a pit . . . and then it was just a small square cellar room. Fragments of crumbled brick lay scattered on the floor, and he swore he saw something white and snake-like disappearing rapidly into the shadows.

"Let's get away from this hole, okay?" he suggested fervently. "Suddenly I don't trust the ground around here very much."

Neither of the others looked likely to object. They retreated towards the station, breathing raggedly. Several passersby gave them distrustful looks, and Bryan realized he must be filthy. He ran a hand through his hair self-consciously.

Stephen was inspecting his left wrist, which already looked swollen. "One of them got you?" Bryan guessed, and Stephen nodded shakily.

"One of what?" Jake asked intensely. Bryan glanced at him, curious.

"What did you see?"

Jake shook his head. "Shadows. It looked like you were very far away for a moment."

"I think we were," Bryan said, breathing out slowly. He noticed that Stephen still hadn't spoken yet. "You okay?"

"Yeah," Stephen said, sounding a little raspy. "I feel like I swallowed a football pitch. I thought we were gonna get *buried* down there. I really . . . I really don't like being under-ground. Did I mention that?"

Bryan patted his shoulder briefly in understanding, and tried not to think too much about the weight of all that earth suddenly closing in from above. . . . Had it been his determination to focus on the reality behind the illusion that had saved them both—or had it been nothing more than sheer luck?

"What *was* that place?" Stephen asked.

Bryan could only shrug, but Jake looked thoughtful.

"I think I remember what used to be here now," he said, frowning. "I *think* this used to be the children's home."

Bryan remembered the doll's shoe they'd found down in the cellar. Pit. Whatever it had been. Somehow, that made everything feel more ominous than it ought to have been, just on the surface. If this had once been a children's home . . . what had happened here?

"That was one of the buildings they knocked down to build the railway?" Stephen asked, but Jake shook his head.

"I read something . . ." His forehead wrinkled. "I don't remember, but I'm sure I read something about a fire. Come on," he said. "Let's get over to my house, and see if I can find the children's home in my books."

"What about the hole?" Stephen asked anxiously. "I mean . . . do we just leave it?"

Bryan hesitated, and then sighed. "We can come back tomorrow, put a board over it or something," he suggested, mostly to stop Stephen from insisting they do something now. He wasn't entirely sure that if they came back the next day, they would even find it. "But I think anybody who's gonna stumble over it . . . is gonna stumble over it whether we cover it over or not." Things in Redford had a habit of being found when the Dark Man *wanted* them to be found.

Stephen still looked uncertain. "I guess . . ." He made Bryan feel obscurely guilty, worrying about the long reach of the Dark Man, all the kids who might come after them. Bryan had spent so long crouching defensively, locked in the events of his own past, that he'd barely stopped to think about the rest of the world.

Another layer of guilt to add to the load. He was always so self-centered—running away without trying to save Adam, fleeing from the Dark Man without trying to warn or protect anybody else . . . Maybe he *deserved* all this that had been heaped on top of him. If he'd been a better brother . . . a better person . . . just *better*—

Familiar pangs of guilt and self-disgust chased each other round and round his head as they made their way to Jake's house.

Jake's parents were still out in the garden. He gave them a quick wave, and hustled his friends inside before too much attention could be drawn to their disheveled appearance. Bryan cleaned himself off as best he could in the pristine bathroom, careful not to leave dirty fingerprints or marks in the sink. It had been a long time since his own house looked as clean as this. The housework that was still done was a cursory pretense more than anything else. Nobody ever visited, anyway.

Bryan emerged, and climbed up to the attic to join the others. Despite himself, he counted steps. *One in fire, two in blood, three in storm and four in flood . . .*

He was relieved to find that there were only ten here. Thirteen steps to the upper floor in King's Hill; thirteen rungs down into the cellar room; thirteen stones out in the woods. The Dark Man's places all bore his number, the sequence that would take you directly to him. The ritual chant as you walked along the pathway into darkness.

Jake was sitting with his knees up, riffling through another thick history book. Stephen was slumped back in the beanbag, still massaging his wrist. "Find anything?" Bryan asked as he sat down.

"Maybe . . . Yes, here." Jake turned the book halfway towards the other two, but then leaned over to look at the pages himself. "I *thought* I remembered reading about it. . . . It was burned down. By one of the boys who used to live there; listen to this." He pulled the book back into his lap to read aloud.

" 'Norton'—that's the boy—'claimed that the orphanage

was a "house of evil," and alleged that the children there had been beaten and maltreated. According to his testimony, staff subjected the children in their care to severe punishments for misbehavior, and rewarded those who brought to light others' misdeeds or revealed their secrets and phobias, which were used to further an atmosphere of control. He made repeated references to an underground chamber used for solitary confinement, but seemed unclear about its exact whereabouts.' " Jake paused to look up at them.

"Yeah. I think we found it," said Bryan quietly.

Jake continued reading. " 'Similarly, although Norton claimed to have witnessed the burial of several children killed during the administration of such brutal punishments, he was unable to lead the authorities to the grave sites. He professed to have been part of a group who secretly returned to mark the site with stones, but such a set of markers was never found, and the dozen other children he named as having taken part in this endeavor denied any such knowledge.' " He turned the page.

" 'It was concluded that Robert Norton was heavily delusional, and hence he was not imprisoned for the arson attack, but sent to a sanatorium outside London, where he remained for several years. The old orphanage building was completely gutted in the fire, and was eventually knocked down to make way for the railway expansion.' "

Jake shut the book with a heavy snap. There was a long silence.

"They're not just steps, they're markers," Bryan said slowly. A trail of stones, leading to a buried secret. Except the secret had stayed buried, those who knew fearfully pretending not to, and those who did dare to speak up disbelieved. The Dark Man's power must have grown up around that horrific beginning, like a pearl forming around grit in an oyster.

A speck of grit in Redford's history. Something that seemed only small, from the outside, but so wrong and out of place that everything about it was buckled and warped.

"So this Pete guy." Stephen spoke up finally. "The one who's supposed to haunt King's Hill. Was *he* the Dark Man? He must have been at the children's home when there were all the murders. . . . Maybe it was his ghost all along."

Bryan shook his head. "I don't think this is one man's ghost," he said flatly. He couldn't imagine that the Dark Man was just a single restless spirit; he was too . . . *big,* somehow, too powerful. Peter Hayward might have seen what happened at the children's home, might have been a part of it . . . but even in his death, he was still only a part of it.

"It's more like . . . the ghost of *what happened,* not just the ghost of a person," Bryan said slowly, feeling it all come together in his head. "We're trapped in their nightmare," he added. "Those kids . . . all those kids, they died here, and what happened to them . . . stayed. The Dark Man is the whole thing brought to life; he knows all your fears, and nobody listens when you try to tell them what's happening."

"What about the rhyme?" Stephen asked.

"What if it started as . . . a way to remember?" Jake suggested softly. "A way to . . . not forget what happened to all the ones who disappeared. And it just got passed down, and down, and down, and probably nobody remembered what it was about or all the original words . . . but things like that always spread. Nobody even remembers how it started any longer, but the legend keeps growing."

"And so does the Dark Man," Bryan finished grimly.

"He must *feed* on the kids he steals," Stephen said, with a look of revulsion. "If he was first created by what happened to those kids, then every one that dies must make him stronger."

Bryan thought of Adam as a trapped soul, helping fuel the very thing that had stolen him away in the first place, and felt a white-hot core of anger beginning to grow in him. The crimes that had been visited on those long-ago helpless kids had echoes beyond the grave, dooming countless others to the same fate. They couldn't just let it go on like this.

But how could they stop it?

"Do you think anyone ever tried to stop it?" Stephen asked, echoing Bryan's thoughts.

"If they did, it didn't work," Bryan said darkly.

"You'd have to go right back to the scene of the crime; the center of it all," Jake said softly. He looked at Bryan. "And that means going to the Devil's Footsteps."

~ XXII ~

"I'M JUST THINKING ABOUT WHAT NINA SAID," Stephen said suddenly, breaking the leaden silence. "Her friend Marcie thought she saw children's ghosts—"

"You think those were actual ghosts?" Bryan asked.

"Maybe . . ." He shrugged. "I should call Nina anyway. She must have heard all the latest stories—she was trying to convince me it was real. . . . She might know something else."

"Okay." Bryan doubted Stephen's sister could help, but he didn't bother trying to argue. He already knew, with a kind of fatalistic despair, what anything they tried was going to come down to.

The Devil's Footsteps. Everything led back to the Devil's Footsteps, sooner or later. Everything led right back into the heart of the woods.

One in fire, two in blood, three in storm and four in flood . . .

Come on, Bryan! What the hell are you so afraid of?

He closed his eyes against the memories, listening to the vague murmur of Stephen's voice as he talked on the phone downstairs. Jake was silent, except for the occasional scrape of the corner of a page as he turned it. Bryan wasn't sure whether he was looking for more on the orphanage, or just reading. He probably wasn't used to having company while he read.

Not since Lucy had disappeared. Bryan wondered how many other people through the years had lost brothers, sisters, friends, children to the thieving hands of the Dark Man. How many of them had ever known or guessed what had happened? Had other people tried to find out how to fight back against it? Or were they all like his parents, trapped in a horrible limbo of waiting for answers that were never going to come?

He heard the door below click, and then Stephen came hammering back up the stairs, fast enough to make both of them sit up in shock.

"I called my house. Nina's not there. Mum thought she was with us." He didn't say any more than that, but he didn't have to. Bryan scrambled to his feet.

"Want to go look for her?"

Stephen rubbed his forehead anxiously. "It's dumb, I know," he said, apologizing, "but—"

"No problem." Jake cut him off quickly.

"I just want to—you know."

"Yeah."

"We understand."

The other two shrugged as if it were nothing, but when Bryan met Jake's eyes, he saw that they were as troubled as his own. Stephen might still be able to tell himself that nothing could happen to Nina, but both of them had reason to have lost that kind of denial. Things *could* happen to your brother, or your best friend, or your little sister . . . and Bryan was suddenly horribly aware of how naïve they'd been.

Did we really think the Dark Man was just gonna sit around and wait for us to plan our next move?

They left Jake's house at speed, spilling out into afternoon sunshine that suddenly didn't seem quite so bright and cheerful as it had a few minutes before. "She'll have gone to Becca's house," Stephen said quickly. "She's round there all the time."

"Yeah." Bryan tried to sound relaxed, casual, but they were walking far too quickly, moving with a kind of unspoken but shared anxiety. The shadows were back in earnest; that feeling like an itch at the back of the neck, the sensation of being watched . . . His heart rose in his throat, and all of a sudden it seemed to him that their footsteps were landing in perfect unison, thumping out a heavy, dangerous beat.

One in fire . . . two in blood . . . three in storm . . . four in flood.

He dragged his feet for a step, desperate to break that toofamiliar rhythm before it could take over his mind again. Jake glanced across at him, but said nothing, quickly looking away.

It's gonna be all right, it's gonna be all right, it's gonna be all right . . . Bryan forced out the Devil's Footsteps rhyme with something like a directionless prayer. But it was an empty mantra, meaningless even as he kept repeating it. *You have to believe* . . . And he didn't, he couldn't make himself. He couldn't make himself believe in happy endings when all he could think of was Adam: Adam's empty room and the silence between his parents and the way the house didn't feel *whole* anymore. . . .

Stephen led them almost at a trot to a house a few streets from his own. "This is Becca's house, she'll be here," he told them, with only the slightest flicker in his expression to betray the illusion of confidence.

He raised a hand to knock, and Bryan was suddenly struck by an image from way back in his memory. His father, knocking on doors; first friends, and then friends of friends, and then anybody at all. *Is Adam here? Have you seen our Adam? Did he come here? Have you seen him?*

Of course, even then Bryan had known in his heart of hearts that the search was pointless. It gave him a strange hollow chill now, to think of it; he wasn't sure if it was the memory that disturbed him, or the question whether, if he went out to face the Dark Man and never came back, his father would do the same for him? Would he rage and cry and hammer on doors? Or had he burned all that out in the search for Adam, until he was left with nothing but the cold gray lifelessness that was all he ever seemed to show?

Bryan was so caught up in memory that he was almost taken by surprise when a youngish blond woman opened the door and smiled out at them. He'd been expecting that strangely shifty expression people had started to wear when the MISSING posters went up and the news reports came out; the look that was pity mixed with relief and the guilt that came with it. *We know your boy's missing, but we're okay, at least it didn't happen to us, at least we're all okay. . . .*

Instead the woman just looked cheerful and mildly surprised. "Stephen, hi! What are you doing out here?"

"Sorry to bother you, Mrs. Cunningham," Stephen said politely. "Did our Nina come round here?"

Mrs. Cunningham smiled, and Bryan had to stop himself

from crying out in relief. *It's not always the Dark Man,* he berated himself. *You're seeing things now, you're paranoid. There still can be perfectly normal explanations.*

"Ah, yes," said Mrs. Cunningham. "She came round about a half hour ago to ask if Becca could come out to play. She wanted to go down to the park, but our Becca's still grounded from last week, so she went by herself. She's probably still down there now." The relief flowing through him abruptly crystallized into something colder than ice. One little girl, casually sauntering off to the park . . .

It's not over yet. Oh God, it's not over yet.

❦ XXIII ❧

"IT'S JUST THE PARK, RIGHT?" said Stephen, for the second, maybe third time. "Kids go down there all the time; kids play there all the time." He left unspoken the suggestion that maybe Nina hadn't just gone down there to play; maybe she'd gone down there to *prove* that the ghosts of Redford were more than just a story. . . .

"Of course they do," Jake said to fill the slightly strained silence, because Bryan couldn't speak. His tongue seemed to have gone completely dry and stuck itself to the inside of his mouth. If he could have spoken, he might have yelled at them that they needed to stop, to go back, they weren't ready for this. It wasn't time to take the battle to the Dark Man yet, they weren't *ready*.

He might have said all that, or he might not. Because even stronger than the suffocating fear was the weight of all his guilt, hoarded up and sharpened and polished every day for the past five years. *You ran away. He came for Adam, and you ran away. You told yourself there was nothing you could do, but you were wrong, weren't you? You could have fought him. If you'd stayed—*

If he'd stayed . . . who knew? Could he have saved Adam, or would he have been taken as well—or instead? What if it *had* been him snatched? Would that have doomed his brother to the same living hell he'd been experiencing these past five years? Part of him was sure of it, but another, deeper, darker part whispered that maybe they would have got over it, if it had been him. Maybe his parents would have recovered from the loss of their younger son, the way they never had from losing Adam. After all, they'd had him longer, he'd always been the smarter one, the braver one, the stronger one. . . .

The bitter taste of those thoughts was all too familiar, a sour chain of might-have-beens that would boil up from the back of his mind in unexpected moments. There were days when he knew in his soul it wasn't true . . . and other, darker, colder days when he couldn't be so sure.

He thought of Stephen, so desperately concerned over Nina. And here they were, rushing into the Dark Man's arms to try and save her. . . . Why hadn't *he* done that? Why couldn't he have been that kind of brother? Why had he just *run away?*

All of this and more blazed trails through his thoughts, twisting up his insides with the force of all the fear and the anger and the guilt and the bitterness. . . . He was heading back to the scene of the crime, and it was all coming back to him.

His palms were slick with sweat and his heart lay heavy in his chest, and nearly all of him was screaming to turn back— nearly all of him, except for the part that recognized how badly scarred and broken these five years had made him, a diamond-hard part that whispered it would rather die before it let this happen to anybody else.

But as they jogged through the Redford streets—not quite running, because running meant admitting that something truly might be wrong—Bryan wanted to laugh at himself. Thinking so dramatically about how he'd rather die . . . well, he knew the truth of that, didn't he? If that was true, he would have turned and faced the Dark Man long before, instead of running away and clinging so desperately to the dismal, battered, pathetic excuse for a life he still had left.

The weight of that knowledge settled heavily on him. He was the weak link in the chain here. Stephen was the one who'd spoken up about what he'd seen, Jake was the one who'd kept investigating what was happening . . . what had *he* ever done, apart from run away? He couldn't do this. And worse, he knew that if he spoke up and warned his companions that he was sure to break at any moment, they wouldn't believe him. They trusted him, and they didn't understand how much of a mistake it was, didn't understand that he was a coward who would cut and run and leave them just as he'd run away and left Adam. . . .

But then they were at the park gates, and there was no more time to speak up about anything.

Bryan had come through there the other day, but he had been blinded by his memories and the terror that Jake might be bleeding to death right in front of him. Now, for the first time, he looked at his surroundings and truly saw them, and the blood in his veins stood still.

The wrought iron gates were exactly as he remembered them, tall and black and imposing.

"The gates are shut," observed Jake softly, and Bryan fancied he heard another voice just beneath it, like an echo; the voice of his ten-year-old self. *The gates are shut, Adam. Why are they shut?* The park gates had always stood open, every single day he could remember . . . except that one.

"They are—but not to keep us out," Bryan said just as quietly. He stepped forward and touched the left-hand gate lightly. It silently fell open as if all that metal weighed nothing at all.

"Point of no return," whispered Jake, and none of them spoke up to tell him not to be stupid. They hesitated together, caught up in the knowledge that once they stepped through those gates, that was it. One way or another, this would come to an end.

Stephen was the one to break the moment. With a determined set to his shoulders, he strode forward. "My sister's in there, somewhere," he said pointedly, and the other two trailed after him.

Stephen and Jake both jumped as the gate swung shut behind them, but Bryan had been expecting it. He did what he hadn't dared to do with Adam watching him scornfully, and rattled it with a hand. He wasn't at all surprised to learn that despite the fact that it had no lock, it was locked.

"Well. That's that, then," said Stephen, and Jake laughed nervously.

"Why are we—? It's not as if we can't climb the gates." The other two both smiled and nodded, but inside Bryan knew that they wouldn't be climbing them, no matter what happened. They would leave by the gates only if the Dark Man relinquished his grip over them . . . one way or another.

They looked out over the park. It was eerily deserted, as

empty as if it were midnight in winter and not a sunny Sunday afternoon. The sun beaming down on the battered play equipment only served to heighten the wrongness of the moment, mockingly pointing out how perfect a day it was for all the children who weren't there.

"Where are the kids?" breathed Stephen softly.

"Maybe they went where the Redford people always go," said Jake.

The town was always suddenly deserted when something was about to happen, but this felt like something different, something more. The rules had changed, and maybe that was their fault. They'd pushed their way into the Dark Man's places of power, tried to fight him, tried to learn his secrets. Now he was pushing back.

"But Nina went into the woods," said Stephen, finally. It wasn't a question. The false bravado had dropped; none of them could pretend there was nothing wrong here any longer. "We have to go after her," he said determinedly. "But how do we—?"

As if in answer to the unfinished question, a child's voice rose up from the trees. Bryan couldn't quite tell if it was one voice or many voices, male or female, and he somehow couldn't make out the words for all that the voice rang clearly through the still air. But that didn't matter, for the rise and fall of the rhythm was all too familiar. A ritual chant, a child's skipping rhyme. It sliced through his brain like a knife, and, just like that, he was five years in the past.

~ XXIV ~

"OH, COME ON, BRYAN." Adam scowled impatiently as his younger brother scuttled to keep up.

"Wait!" pleaded Bryan. His legs were short compared to his brother's, and going down to the park with Adam wasn't like walking with Mum and Dad. Adam was supposed to be looking out for his little brother, but he preferred to run on ahead, darting across the streets without the slightest fear of traffic and expecting Bryan to do the same.

Adam was never afraid of anything, and Bryan hated that because it meant he had to be the same. Embarrassing yourself in front of your schoolmates came and went, but show yourself up in front of Adam and he'd remember it *forever*.

"C'mon, we have to hurry! Mum'll be here soon."

At twelve years old, Adam was far too old to have parents hanging around the whole time, cramping his style. Their corner of Redford was a quiet enough little place, and they were allowed to ride their bikes or go down to the park if they stuck together, but their mother didn't like to go too long without checking on them. Bryan thought that was okay compared to some people's parents he knew, but to Adam it was criminally restrictive.

Bryan was still—although he'd never admit it—a little nervous about being out alone. Not because he was scared, but because he was sure Adam was going to do something stupid or crazy, and how was he supposed to stop him? Now, as he chased his brother downhill towards the park, he was troubled by the sight of the wrought iron gates barring their way.

"The gates are shut, Adam. Why are they shut?"

Adam made a "duh, how thick are you?" face. " 'Cause somebody shut them?" He reached for the nearest gate to give it a push, but Bryan hung back.

"I don't know, Adam," he said uneasily. "What if the park's closed or something?"

Adam sneered at that with the full force of his twelve years of worldly wisdom. "No one's gonna close the *park*, Bry. Come *on*." He shoved the gates open in a rattle of metal, and Bryan didn't have any choice but to follow.

His unease deepened to near panic as he saw that the park was completely empty. No parents with babies, no other kids, no teenagers playing football . . . it was as if they were the only two people left in the world. He grabbed his brother by the arm.

"It *is* closed, Adam, I told you!"

"It's *not*!" Adam scowled, shaking him off. "And who cares if it is? We've got the whole place to ourselves." He grinned suddenly, wickedly pleased with himself. "Let's go into the *woods*," he said.

"Adam, we can't!" Bryan objected. They weren't allowed in the woods on their own. And he didn't want to, anyway. He hated the woods.

His brother's voice became more sneakily persuasive. "Come on, Bry, let's go into the woods," he begged. "Come on, it'll be so cool. What are you afraid of, Bryan? Mum and Dad won't even know. We can sneak in and be back before they come and get us. What are you afraid of?"

Plenty, but nothing Bryan could explain to his brother. "They'll be here any second," he said instead.

"No they won't, we've got *ages*." Adam casually shot him down. He allowed his mouth to curl into a mocking grin. "You're not *chicken*, are you?"

There was only one possible answer to that.

"No!"

Adam grinned wider. "Well, come on, then!" He sprinted off towards the woods. And Bryan followed. Because . . . well, what else?

Bryan had never been in the woods before without his parents, and he didn't like it much at all. Even in the bright sunlight, there was something menacing about the way the trees seemed to close in on you, funneling you in one direction so you went where the trees wanted you to, not where *you* wanted to.

But he couldn't exactly tell Adam that the trees were out to get them. *That* he'd be hearing about until he was a hundred and two. Instead he whined, "Adam, where are we *going*?"

"Getting scared, are you?"

"No! I just—" Bryan stopped abruptly as he nearly ran into his brother. "What is it?" His voice came out higher than he'd have liked, with an edge of panic, but for once Adam didn't notice.

"It's just some kind of clearing or—oh, *wow!*" Adam's entire face lit up. Bryan squeezed past him, and then his jaw dropped. There, right in front of them in the long, ragged grass, was a trail of stones leading round in a snaking path. He didn't have to count them to know how many there would be. Thirteen stones. *Thirteen steps to the Dark Man's door . . .*

"Oh, wow!" said Adam again. "It's really *real!*"

"Let's get out of here, Adam," Bryan said. His heart was so tight in his chest that he almost didn't care if he sounded like a total wimp.

But Adam wouldn't be swayed. "Are you kidding?" He hopped onto the first stone, and jumped off and on again with a grin. Bryan winced. "It's just like everybody says! One in fire, two in—"

"Adam!" he yelped. He could feel it; something building, some dark power growing as his brother casually played with something far, far too dangerous. . . .

Adam dropped down from the stone and turned to grin at him. His eyes were so lit up that for a moment they almost glowed, and Bryan took an involuntary step backwards. "You're *scared,*" Adam said, smirking.

Of course I am, I should be scared, we both should, can't you feel it?

"No I'm not!"

"Then I dare you. I dare you to do the rhyme."

And Bryan was caught. Refusing a dare was the worst thing *ever.* Adam would spread it all around the school, he knew it. For the rest of his life, he'd be the kid who found the Devil's Footsteps and was *too scared* to say the rhyme.

His life wouldn't be worth living.

"I'll do it."

"Go on, then." And Adam just stood there grinning, as if it were nothing, as if it were just some stupid little game and not the deadliest thing ever.

But Bryan had taken the dare, and there was no backing out now.

Before he could lose his nerve, Bryan closed his eyes and took the first step forwards. In a rush of dizziness, it felt as though he were not merely standing on a flat rock in the grass, but atop some great cliff, a few thousand feet high.

He didn't want to say the words aloud, didn't want to call upon that magic power, but they echoed inside his head all the same. The internal chant kept time with Adam's mocking voice, sounding at one and the same time as if it came from a few feet away and far, far below.

One in fire. The rhythm of the chant bound him, forcing him to move onwards when he didn't want to. *Two in blood*. Against his own will, his feet kept going. *Three in storm . . . four in flood*. Now the voice that chanted alongside the one in his head didn't sound like Adam at all, but altogether deeper, darker, and nastier.

Five in anger . . . six in hate . . . seven fear . . . evil eight.

Bryan felt as if he were frozen with fear, but he couldn't be, because he was still moving. His eyes were jammed shut, and he no longer dared to even think of opening them for fear of what he might see. His lips curled back from his teeth in a grimace of terror, but he still couldn't stop himself.

Nine in sorrow . . . ten in pain . . . eleven death—

He let out an uncontrollable squeak at that ominous eleventh step, and his eyes flew open. A cold jolt of terror snapped him out of his near trance. What was he doing? This wasn't just a dare, it was life and death. What could Adam do to him, that was worth facing down the Dark Man?

Suddenly, in thinking that, Bryan had control of his own body again. Before the terrible hypnotic power of the chant had a chance to wash back over him, he wrenched himself away from following the pathway, and jumped.

For a moment he was falling, falling . . . And then he was just standing on the ground, because after all, the steps were just stones, a couple of inches high. Weren't they?

The last remnants of the echoing chant were washed away by Adam's scornful laughter. Bryan didn't care about that. He could feel the darkness in this place, a pulsing, terrible sense of evil that was growing with every second. It filled the air, choking him, until he could barely breathe or see or think. . . .

He started to run for the safety of the trees, for their last chance at escape. Maybe it wasn't too late, maybe if he hadn't completed the ritual, the Dark Man wouldn't notice them. . . . He grabbed for his brother's arm, thinking that surely *now* Adam must feel it, but Adam just danced out of the way, still laughing.

"I can't *believe* you!" he laughed. "You're such a wuss! Oh, man, you totally chickened out!"

"Adam! Please! We gotta *go*—" Bryan jiggled up and down desperately in the gap between the trees, knowing that if they didn't run now, something terrible would happen at any moment. *Come on, Adam, please come* on—

But Adam wasn't listening. With a mocking grin, he hopped up backwards onto the first of the steps. "I'm gonna show you how a *real* man takes a dare, Bry. Follow me—come on, kid, I'll go first. If anything comes to get us, it'll get me first, right? Come on, Bryan!" He took another long backward step. "What the hell are you so afraid of?" Step. "You don't seriously *believe* this junk, do you?" Step. "You think the Dark Man's gonna come and get me?"

Bryan was barely even hearing his taunting words. He wanted to scream to his brother that he didn't get it, he didn't *understand*, but he couldn't force the words out. Instead he found himself backing slowly away through the trees as he whispered aloud the words he didn't want to think, the words of power that summoned the Dark Man to collect his sacrifice.

Nine in sorrow . . . ten in pain . . . eleven death . . . twelve life again . . .

~ XXV ~

WITH AN EFFORT, BRYAN SHOOK HIMSELF free of his memories. He didn't want to think about that now; didn't want to think about how he'd been frozen with terror, unable to run after his brother, grab him, drag him, pull him away to safety . . . Didn't want to think about how his last-ever glimpse of his brother had been that terrified split second as Adam turned to face the unfolding form of the Dark Man . . . and Bryan turned to run for his life.

He ran a shaky hand through his sweaty hair, focusing on the park, forcing himself back into the present. The eerie rise and fall of the chant continued, turning what should have been a perfectly ordinary sunlit scene into something immeasurably more creepy. He looked across at the others, and found them both watching him.

"Bryan?" asked Jake quietly.

Bryan gave a brisk nod in reply. "Let's do this."

They walked together towards the trees. Bryan fancied he could feel the world stretching and bulging out of shape, so that the looming woods became huge, and everything else behind them and beside them was shrinking down into nothingness. Yet these woods didn't feel alien, they felt like Redford—smelled like it, the stench of something that had died a long time ago, and just been left to rot.

He thought of the children from the orphanage. They'd been killed and buried in secret, hidden away so thoroughly that even when the tale was told it wasn't believed . . . but not without a trace. Whatever had happened here so long ago had left a stain on the history of the town so strong it kept spreading outwards.

They walked on into the woods. Bryan could hear the eerie rise and fall of the chant up ahead, unquestionably in the rhythm of the words he knew so well, and yet still indistinct.

"Do you know where we're going?" asked Jake, voice barely more than a whisper. They all felt the urge to stay hushed, but it wasn't the respectful silence that settled over a graveyard or some ancient place of power—rather, the tense, fearful quiet of knowing that there was *something out there.*

"Of course I do." Bryan spoke with absolute conviction. He knew it in his blood and under his skin. For the past five years it had been there, haunting his days and filling his nightmares, the silent call to return to this place. If he'd been suddenly struck blind and deaf, he still would have found it. Or it would have found him.

Stephen let out his breath in an abrupt gasp as a shape loomed out of the shadows. And then he relaxed. "Nina!" He made to step towards her, but Bryan yanked him back.

Nina looked up at them, and smiled innocently. But her eyes were completely blank, flat and white with no humanity in them. She silently beckoned them to follow.

"What—?" Stephen stood frozen, caught between seeing his sister's familiar face and seeing the alien nature those blank eyes betrayed.

"It's the Dark Man," said Bryan quietly. "He's in control now. His rules. So let's follow."

Jake sucked in a sharp breath, but said nothing. The girl who wasn't quite Nina led the way in complete silence. Bryan realized suddenly that the chant they'd been hearing all this time had cut out; and yet somehow its absence was even worse. The only sounds were the footsteps and the breathing of the three boys. Literally the *only* sounds—there was no wind, no birdsong, and though Nina walked the same path they did, her footsteps were silent.

It wasn't a noise that made Bryan suddenly look to the side, then, but maybe some movement at the corner of his eye, or maybe just a prickle of a feeling. Child-sized shadows rippled through the trees to either side of the path, as if the four of them were marching in step with an invisible host. The dappled sunlight that made it through the thick network of branches should never have been able to cast them.

Beside him, Jake's breath hitched, and Bryan knew that he had noticed the shadows too. By a common agreement that didn't need to be spoken out loud, Jake gripped him by the wrist. On the other side, Stephen did the same; just about the closest you could get to holding hands without looking like that was what you were doing. Not that appearances really mattered, here and now.

Their unnatural escort led them on through the woods.

The journey seemed to take a long time, but Bryan wasn't fooled. The route they traveled could be just as long or as short as the Dark Man chose to make it.

All this waiting, all this ceremony—it was all to allow the chill trickle of fear to build in his chest. He *knew* that, understood that, but it was working all the same. The Dark Man might be trying to frighten him, but that didn't mean the fear wasn't justified.

I'm crazy, we're all crazy. What are we doing? Why had they ever been crazy enough to think they could come to the forest and do this? Whatever "this" was. They had no more idea now how to defeat the Dark Man than they had when they'd begun this. And now there was no more time for thinking.

The woods around him started to look familiar—so familiar, Bryan wasn't sure if he was still in the present, or locked in the details of that day that had been imprinted on his memory forever. There was the twisted root he had stumbled over, there was the tree with the gnarled trunk that looked as if it were leaning over to peer down at him . . . And there, *there* . . . The clearing.

If it hadn't been for Jake and Stephen beside him, he might have stopped dead then and there, slamming into the weight of five years of nightmares. It didn't just look the same as it had, it *was* the same. The world seemed to go spinning dizzily out of control, everything he had seen and done and felt for the past five years fading away into nothing more than a fevered dream. And then Stephen tightened his grip on his arm, and said quietly, "Bryan?"

And the moment was gone.

Bryan took a deep, shaky breath, and stepped forwards. Their silent escort fell back, and Jake and Stephen released his arms, as if they knew instinctively they'd reached a point that was his alone to pass beyond.

And there it was, that simple little snaking trail of stones. Stone markers, for the graves of children whose names nobody remembered. Thirteen steps, just tiny little jumps like a hopscotch game. It would take no effort at all to walk from one end to the other . . . and yet, it would take everything.

The Devil's Footsteps.

Bryan closed his eyes for a long moment. Images, memories swirled in the dark behind his eyelids. He breathed, slowly, until the dark was all there was, and then he opened them again.

The world seemed to have shrunk, or perhaps it was just that he was seeing nothing but what was directly before him. He was aware of Stephen and Jake and the silent Nina, but only distantly, as if they were the crowd far up in the stands and he stood alone in the center of the football pitch. And it was down to him to make the kickoff.

He stepped forwards.

XXVI

THE WORLD AROUND HIM BUCKLED AND CHANGED. All of a sudden the stillness of the forest glade was shattered as it transformed into a nightmare landscape of black, cracked earth and burning trees. The heat was so intense that his skin began to blister; he felt as if it were *melting.* . . . He let out a yell, suddenly wholly convinced he'd been transported directly into hell.

It's over, you're dead, you totally screwed up, and I guess this is what happens to boys who leave their brothers to die—

And then he thought—*One in fire.* This wasn't hell. Hell was a trail of stones away. This was only the first step.

And he moved forward.

The clearing snapped back to its previous appearance, and Bryan let out a quick sigh of relief. He was here, he was fine, he was doing it. He'd passed the first test.

But not unscathed. His skin still itched fiercely with the force of the heat that had baked it, and even though he knew he shouldn't, he had to go for the temporary relief of rubbing his arms to soothe them.

His skin felt strange, loose under his questing fingertips. He looked down at his arms, and screamed in terror. His skin was blackened and cracked, oozing with thick, dark blood. Heart's blood. He stood in a kind of numb trance, watching as his life pumped away out of the arteries in his ruined arms. In a matter of minutes, he would surely be dead. . . .

One in fire, two in blood. Two in blood. It's not real.

It is real.

Even as he realized that this was the second phase of the test, that knowledge rang hollow in his mind. The things the Dark Man did—were they real, or were they not? He didn't know, and it didn't matter, because they could still kill you. And how could he possibly move, when he was standing here watching himself bleed to death, the energy seeping out of him with the last of his waning life force . . . ?

No! He wasn't sure if the shout of defiance sounded only in his head, but it rang in his ears just the same. He bit his bottom lip, fiercely, trying to cut through the terrible overwhelming numbness. Blood for blood, wasn't that how it worked? As the thin trickle ran its way down his chin, suddenly he could move again.

He took another step.

Three in storm.

His arms were his own again, clean and whole, the skin reddened as if with sunburn—or perhaps only from his own rubbing. All of a sudden the world had grown dark, and huge globules of cold rain pelted down. His hair flattened against his head and his clothes grew heavy with the sheer weight of water smashing down from the sky. It was coming so fast and so thickly that it *hurt*, that same solid impact you got from crashing into the surface of a swimming pool at the wrong angle.

Bryan started to move, and the world exploded in a flash of sound and light. Weren't you supposed to judge the distance of the lightning by the gap before the thunder? There was no gap at all—it must have missed him by inches. As the purple blotches in his vision faded, he could see that the stones ahead of him had completely disappeared, blasted out of existence by the force of the thunderbolt. The wet air crackled with static, and it smelt like train tracks.

The path was destroyed. He couldn't go forward, and if he stood here for a second longer he might as well just be a lightning conductor. He was going to have to—

Turn back? No. No, he couldn't. If he did that, everything was lost. And yet, if the steps were destroyed . . .

But how could they be? The steps were part of the Dark Man, part of his power, the route to the center of it. Surely they couldn't truly be destroyed until the moment he was?

Acting on impulse, Bryan closed his eyes. Even though his brain was telling him urgently that he was going to fall, he stepped forward. He staggered, almost fell . . . and then he was on the next step.

One fire, two in blood, three in storm and four in flood . . .

Hey, I can do this. The solution was simple; why hadn't he thought of it before? All he had to do was keep his eyes closed and not believe anything his senses tried to tell him. . . .

Bryan cried out in shock as his feet were suddenly swept

from under him, and his knees hit the rock with a violent crack. He grasped desperately for the slippery stone as water rose around him, black as midnight and smelling as if it came from a sewer full of dead things. He gagged at the stench of it, and fought to keep his head above the surface as it surged around him, trying to wrench him from the step he clung to so desperately.

His head was going under . . . the thought of getting that stuff in his *mouth*, swallowing it . . .

He dared to release the stone with one hand long enough to clap it over his nose, and almost slid off into the water. With a wordless howl of disgust behind his hand, he threw himself down under the surface and scrabbled for the next rock.

He found it, and then the water was gone. He straightened up, spluttering and coughing, dry but with the scent of filth still clinging to his body. *Five in anger . . .*

This wasn't fair. What had he ever done to deserve this? Why should all this suddenly be resting on *his* shoulders?

Decade after decade of disappearing kids. All of a sudden somebody had to take a stand, and it had to be him? Who'd picked Bryan Holden's name out of the lottery? Now he was going to get killed out here—wasn't losing one son enough for his parents?

But why should he care about them? They didn't care about him. Nobody cared what happened to him, so why should he care about anybody else?

For a moment he thought of Stephen's desperation over Nina, but only for a moment. Why should Stephen get to have someone swoop in and rescue his sister? No one had done that for him when it had been Adam. He'd gone through hell for five years—why should it suddenly be up to him to make sure other people didn't suffer?

They wanted him to take a stand now? Well, he was taking one. He was taking a stand against the universe in general, and every injustice that had brought him to this point. He was walking away. He was . . .

Running away.

I can't believe you! You're such a wuss! Oh, man, you totally chickened out!

Adam's voice echoed in his head, and suddenly the white-hot flame of his anger turned inwards. Didn't deserve this? Of course he deserved this. None of this would ever have happened if he hadn't been a coward in the first place. If he hadn't chickened out on those last two steps and forced Adam to take his place on the road to doom. It was *all* his fault, every bit of it.

The tide of fury at his own uselessness swept over him, and somewhere in the middle of it, he took another step.

Six in hate.

The flame of self-hatred burned, igniting five years of guilt and self-disgust. What was he doing here? Did he think he was supposed to be some kind of hero? He was nothing but a coward; that was the real truth. That was who he really was.

He was still the same boy he'd been five years before; the boy who'd stood by and let Adam follow the Footsteps, knowing what it meant for him. The boy who'd turned and run away, not even *waiting* to see what happened to his brother, not even *trying* to save him from the Dark Man's clutches.

The boy who'd seen what was happening to his parents, and never said a word. The boy who saw how the kids were still disappearing, and never lifted a finger to stop it. The boy who'd never even *thought* of trying to fight the Dark Man until Stephen and Jake had come along and told him to.

The boy who was still Adam Holden's little brother, and still had a job to do.

He took another step.

XXVII

FIVE IN ANGER, SIX IN HATE . . . That made this the seventh step. The halfway mark. Halfway to meeting the Dark Man on his home ground. *Seven fear . . .*

I'm already half dead.

He didn't want to die! He didn't want to move. He didn't want to finish this.

Better surely just to stay frozen here in the middle. Unable to go back, unwilling to go forwards . . . Just as he'd been frozen ever since Adam disappeared. Trapped outside of time in a world where it felt as if none of them were living.

And shouldn't he feel that he would rather die than live like that? But he didn't. He might have only a bitter slice of the life he'd once had, but he was hanging on to it grimly with both hands. He was afraid to let go.

Afraid to let go, even to grasp at the chance of something

better. If he wanted to escape, then he *had* to let go. Even if that meant the fear of falling.

He took another step.

Evil eight.

The dark descended so suddenly that Bryan truly feared he'd gone blind. The space closed in around him, and he sensed he was trapped, down in the dark, utterly alone. . . .

You're still in the woods.

Was he still in the woods? On some level, perhaps, but he was in the Dark Man's domain now. Perhaps everything he met was nowhere but in his own head . . . but that didn't mean it wasn't real.

He reached out his hands, and met brick walls. Abruptly, he knew where he was. He was under the earth, down under the old orphanage, with the air running out and the walls closing in and nowhere to run or hide. . . .

He looked up, but no sunlight spilled in to alleviate the darkness. The boards they had broken to get in had been re-placed; or perhaps here they'd never been broken at all. This was the underground chamber in another time and place, someone else's memory.

This was the underground chamber when you were down there in the dark, waiting for someone to come and get you.

He could hear labored breathing, and he wasn't sure it was his own. Was he alone down in the dark? He was afraid to find out.

Was this the next step? How could he step anywhere? He was trapped, he couldn't move, and *something* was coming . . .

It didn't matter if the something had a name, or a shape, because down here in the dark it made no difference, down here in the dark it was just a faceless, featureless evil coming to get you. All your fears, given shape.

The Dark Man.

There was a creak of hinges as the trapdoor was thrown open, but it let in no light, only cold, rank air. Every instinct in him was urging him to shrink back, to hide . . . but there was nowhere to go. He could only wait, huddled in fear, for the Dark Man to come and get him.

No, that wasn't true. There was one more choice; he could go *up* before it came down, and face the Dark Man on his own terms.

No more cowering. He'd been waiting for the Dark Man to come and get him for the past five years; it was time to stop cowering down in the dark. He stepped forward, reached for the unseen rungs of the ladder he knew would be there, and hauled himself up—

—Back into the light.

Five in anger, six in hate, seven fear and evil eight. Nine in sorrow . . .

The sunlight was blinding, it brought stinging tears to his eyes. And once they'd started flowing, he couldn't seem to make them stop.

When was the last time he'd truly cried? Bryan was shaken to find that he couldn't even remember. He hadn't shed a single tear over Adam. His brother had been wrenched away from his world so quickly and completely there was no room for grieving in the chaos that followed. And afterwards . . . well, how could he cry afterwards, when he never had before?

Adam hadn't even had a funeral. Funerals were for people who died, not those who were just *gone*. Bryan might know his brother wasn't coming back, but his parents didn't have that certainty, and maybe that was eating away at them even more than it ate at him. If you didn't have a funeral, you didn't have an end . . . and without an end it just went on and on forever, never changing, never getting any better.

He was crying now, but he didn't feel any relief; only a never-ending well of grief being dredged up from the center of himself. Grief for Adam. For his parents. For himself. For all the others—

All the others.

He suddenly looked up through his haze of tears, but the clearing was empty of everyone but himself. He was alone.

No, you idiot, you're not on your own. They're there. You can't see them, but you know they're there. Jake and Stephen, waiting for him, trusting in him. Nina, taken over by the Dark Man and waiting for him, him alone, to walk the path—and, one way or another, to break the spell.

So for God's sake, don't just stand there crying about it!

And he took another step forward.

Ten in pain.

The racking sobs that had overcome him subsided into heaving breaths, each one seeming to threaten to rip his insides out of him. His heart was hammering away at the inside of his rib cage so fiercely that he thought it was going to explode.

Oh my God, I'm actually having a heart attack.

Bryan fell to his knees, clutching his chest even though the pain went further than that now. He wanted to crawl away from the Footsteps, jump down and surrender—anything to make it stop.

Until he thought, *What pain? This pain?* This pain was

161

only physical, it was his body under torture, not his mind and his feelings and the whole center of himself. Wasn't he used to living in pain? So he ought to be more than able to take this.

Thinking wasn't doing, but in this place of challenges, strength of will meant everything. He forced himself to his feet, and pushed forward through a barrier of pain so tangible it felt like a wall.

And then it was gone.

He stood for a moment, breathing heavily. The world was eerily still and silent; where was the next challenge? He knew he hadn't come through thirteen steps. He risked closing his eyes for a moment, and mentally counted.

One in fire, two in blood.
Three in storm and four in flood.
Five in anger, six in hate.
Seven fear and evil eight.
Nine in sorrow, ten in pain.
Eleven death—

His eyes flew open. The eleventh step. The death step. His step, the one where he had lost his nerve and fled five years before. *The buck stops here.* Except . . .

There was nothing. No sourceless pain, no dangerously real illusions. No external force gripping hold of his emotions and turning them against him. Nothing. Nothing to prevent him from just moving onwards, and passing on to the next step.

Bryan started to move—and screamed.

Adam's corpse stared sightlessly up at him. It was like that nightmare in the room at the top of the house on King's Hill, only a million times worse. That had been a shadowy, barely glimpsed scene of horror, but this . . . this was Adam. More vivid than any memory or waking dream, more finely detailed than a photograph.

After that first instant of complete and utter shock, Bryan was thrown by the peacefulness of the scene. His brother's still form looked completely at rest; except for the open eyes, he could have been sleeping.

Bryan didn't know how long he stood there. A tiny fraction of a second? A few million years? What was time, in a world where nothing moved and no one lived?

I'm alive. He told himself so, but it didn't seem to mean anything, didn't seem to matter. He felt beautifully lethargic, as if he were on the edge of that Sunday-morning state where you were lying in your sunny bedroom, knowing that any second sleep would come back to claim you.

I don't have mornings like that, when was the last time I had a morning like that?

It was hard to resist the allure of that unfamiliar peace. Why not just let it take him, sink into that numbness and truly rest for the first time in years?

Well, what was so bad about that? Why would it be such a terrible thing to just surrender, and—

You're not chicken, are you?

I'm gonna show you how a real man takes a dare, Bry. Follow me—come on, kid, I'll go first.

Bryan's eyes flickered open, and it was only then that he realized they'd been closed. He saw the world around him, saw it clearly, instead of through the hypnotic haze he'd been drifting in. And he saw Adam.

What did it matter, if he looked peaceful? It wasn't truly

Adam, just the shell he'd left behind; his brother was gone. His brother was dead. Twelve years old and dead. And there was nothing right about that.

He had to go on—and that meant stepping over Adam's body. He screwed his eyes shut . . . Then he opened them again. This wasn't something to be blocked out and ignored, something to pretend away. It ought to be more than that. He owed Adam more than that. He had to pass his brother's corpse if he was going to continue on his road—but he didn't have to do it easily or lightly.

"I'm sorry, Adam," he said quietly, and bowed his head. Then he walked over to his brother's body, and stepped over it.

And Adam's corpse reached up, and grabbed him by the leg.

BRYAN SCREAMED, THE SOUND SHATTERING any last remnant of peace the scene possessed. He backed away in disbelief as his brother sat up. Adam stretched, catlike, and snickered.

"Man, I really got you there, Bry." He grinned. "I got you good!"

Bryan backed away from him, instinctively, eyes wide with shock. "A-Adam?" he stuttered out.

"B-Bryan?" Adam mocked him back. "Hey, what's up?" He moved in on his brother, laughing at the way Bryan scrambled out of his way. "Hey, relax, I'm not gonna bite!"

"You're dead!" Bryan exclaimed.

"I know!" Adam shouted back. His face contorted in the fury that Bryan had always known had to be there, the dark rage at the terrible fate he'd been abandoned to. "You killed me!"

"I—I—" Bryan didn't know what to say. What was he supposed to say? He couldn't say, "That's not true!" could he?

Because it *was* true. He'd left his brother to die, and it was all his fault.

"You left me to *die*, Bryan!" Adam shouted at him. "You knew he was coming for me and you *ran away*. How could you do that to me?"

"I, I, I didn't mean to—"

"You didn't *mean* to?" Adam demanded in disbelief. " 'Whoops, sorry, accidentally killed you there'?"

"It wasn't me!" Bryan shouted back. "It *wasn't* my fault!"

"You knew it was gonna happen! Did you try and stop it? Did you try and help me? No! You just *ran away*. You just ran away and left me!"

"I told you! I warned you!"

"It was a *skipping rhyme*, Bryan! It was a stupid *skipping* rhyme! How was I supposed to know it was real?"

"Well, how was I?" Bryan shot right back, on the defensive.

"But you *did*," Adam said pointedly, holding his hands out imploringly. "You knew, Bryan. You felt it. And you didn't say anything." His tone had changed, and Bryan felt his own reflexive fury drain away, leaving him feeling empty.

"You wouldn't have believed me," Bryan said pleadingly. What was he begging for? Forgiveness, understanding? He didn't know. "You would have just laughed at me."

"I would have *laughed*?" Adam snorted, a bitter, hollow sound. "You didn't try to save my life because I *would have laughed*?"

Bryan closed his eyes. "You wouldn't have believed me," he said again, with all the quiet conviction he had left.

When he opened his eyes again, Adam was looking up at him—up, because Bryan was the taller of them now—and shaking his head sadly. "What—what . . ." He moved away, pushing his straggly blond hair back in a gesture that was achingly familiar. "What do you want me to say, Bryan? What do you think I can possibly say?"

"I . . ." Bryan looked at his feet. "I don't know." He shrugged, and laughed, a shallow, broken sound. "Honest to God, I don't know."

Adam sighed. "Why did you come here, Bryan?" he asked, sounding resigned instead of angry now. And that hurt even worse.

"For . . ." Bryan trailed off. There had been an answer to that question once, hadn't there? Reasons, a purpose, something he was sure of. Looking into his brother's face for the first time in five years, all that had faded away.

"You don't know." Adam smiled faintly in cynical amusement, and sat down.

"Why are *you* here?" Bryan found himself asking.

Adam spread his hands in a shrug and indicated himself. "I got nowhere else to be, Bry."

"But you're . . . but you're dead. You're gone. Passed on."

"I'm not passing anywhere, buddy, I'm stuck right here."

"Stuck . . ." Bryan's jaw tightened. "The Dark Man." The steel of his resolve began to return as he remembered the true reason for his return to the woods.

"Him . . . and you," Adam told him quietly.

"Me? Adam, I didn't, I—"

"I'm not really dead, Bry," his brother told him. "You know that. The Dark Man's got no power, not if you don't give it to him. He makes the world that you believe in. And you don't believe I'm really dead."

"I *know* you are," Bryan objected. Of course he knew it; he

167

knew it in every breath, every nightmare, every second of memory. Every footstep that could no longer be taken without the Dark Man's rhyme returning to him.

"You know it." Adam shrugged and smiled. "But you don't believe it."

"I believe it," he said slowly.

"And yet you're standing here talking to me."

"You're . . . you're not—"

"Not what? Not real?" Adam asked mildly. "Can't believe you still believe in real and not real, after everything that's happened. You should know better."

Bryan frowned. "What . . . what do you mean?"

"What's real, Bry?" Adam asked. "Me, you? The Dark Man? This clearing? Any of it?"

"I'm real," said Bryan, although it was the only one on that list he could be truly confident of.

"You mean you *think* you're real."

"Isn't that enough?"

Adam snorted. "Okay, we'll say you're real. What about the rest of it?" He leaned forward. "Tell me what's real, Bryan."

Bryan saw his own face reflected in the eyes of his brother. The two were an echo, even more alike than they'd been five years ago. He wondered if his parents had seen the resemblance. He wondered if it hurt.

He closed his eyes for a moment, feeling a desperate urge to block it all out for just a second. "I'm real," he repeated, more firmly. He opened his eyes again. "And this is real." He looked around at the clearing. "Maybe not what we see, but . . . everything. What happened. That's real. You were here, and then you were gone, and maybe that's partly my fault or maybe it isn't, but you *were* gone. And you're never coming back."

168

Adam smiled slightly. "So that's reality, is it? Sounds like a fun place to live."

"It's been a barrel of laughs," said Bryan dryly.

"So make it different."

"I can't," he snapped, frowning.

"Sure you can." Adam held out his hand, palm upwards. "This is the Dark Man's place, Bryan. He decides what's gonna be real. I'm part of his world now. If you kill him, you kill me forever."

Bryan shook his head, a short, sharp gesture of denial. "You're already dead."

"I don't have to be. He bends reality, but *you* get to shape it. You can make it different. You can make it so it was *always* different. He makes the whole world look away from Redford, you think he can't do the same for you and me?"

His hand was still held out, unwavering. Bryan looked at him, silent, unmoving.

"Take my hand, Bryan. Take my hand and walk away, and it can all be like it never was. Just take my hand."

Bryan looked at him. And Adam smiled.

XXIX

ADAM'S EYES WERE HUGE in the glowing sunlight. His lips were slightly parted in a mischievous smile, the one that always made you grin right back even though you knew it meant he was plotting some kind of trouble.

And Bryan looked at his outstretched hand, and thought, *It can all be like it never was.*

Would it really be that easy? Was this his prize for coming here and facing down the Dark Man?

Facing down the Dark Man? When did you do that? You haven't finished—

He didn't need to finish. He'd come here to lay the memories of his brother to rest, and instead he'd found something greater, something it would never have occurred to him to hope for. The chance to put the clock back and change those five years to the way they ought to have been.

Five years without the guilt and the nightmares and the

jumping at shadows. Five years with parents who remembered things, who *cared*, who acted as if they were alive. Five years growing up with Adam.

It was such a fragile fantasy that he hardly dared imagine it for fear he might break it. A world where Adam's room was a place you were shouted at for entering, not a warped kind of museum with everything in boxes. A world where Adam's old bike in the garage had been casually tossed out, because after all, it was only a bike. Maybe there would be a new one in its place, a racer, fit for a boy of seventeen.

He and Adam would have been at school together. Adam would be at college, thinking about his A-levels—except Adam *wouldn't* be thinking about them, because he never did. And there'd be homework, and the two of them would both be at the table at eight o'clock in the morning, furiously scribbling maths answers over their Cheerios because they hadn't done them the night before. There wouldn't be any homework done the night before, because Bryan wouldn't *need* to do it—he wouldn't need that excuse to hide himself away in his bedroom, that desperate search for anything at all that might stave off the dark thoughts.

He and Adam would always have better things to do than homework, even if they were stuck indoors. They'd probably have a computer, or the latest games console, because their parents would still care about things like Christmas presents and birthday presents.

The house would never be silent as the grave, because Adam had never been able to deal with silence. He'd have music—some kind of loud, pulsing music, probably chart stuff because Adam was in with the in crowd. And Bryan would have his own music too, and he wouldn't use his headphones to block the world out like he did now; he'd increase the volume to compete with Adam until their parents yelled at them both to turn it down.

Their parents would shout up the stairs for them to come for dinner the way they always used to, instead of his father's quiet, unassuming shuffle to his bedroom door. There would be four places at the dinner table, and a person to fill each of them. They would never eat in silence, but in a storm of continual chatter, stupid jokes, and moans and groans about the dreadful days they'd all had.

Except they would never be *really* dreadful days, because he knew what those were like, and in his world with Adam there wouldn't be any.

Most of all, with his brother by his side again he'd never be so completely isolated as he had been. For five years he'd drifted through the world like a ghost, seeing people, even talking to people, but not *touching* them, not really connecting with them. Other people lived in the world, but Bryan was only passing through, unable to find any kind of anchor, anything to make him solid again. In all that time, he'd never felt any more alive than Adam was.

Not all that time. He remembered, almost with a start, that the past few days had been different. He'd met Stephen and Jake, people who were bound to him, people who lived in the same half-real world as he did. There had been laughter, and sparks, and the adrenaline of actually *doing* something, having a goal, something to fight for.

He felt a pang, but then he reminded himself that there was no reason *that* had to go away. It wasn't as if taking back Adam would make them disappear. If they remembered him in his new, Adam-occupied world, they'd still be his friends, they'd be happy for him. And if they didn't remember . . . well, he could make friends with them again. Somehow he knew instinctively it would be easy, this time around.

Adam was still looking at him, eyebrows cocked in a faintly quizzical look. Bryan's heart was suddenly grasped by the fear that if he thought too long over this offer, it might be cruelly snatched away from him, and he raised his hand to take Adam's . . .

And stopped.

"What?" said Adam, sounding more surprised and amused than irritated with him.

And Bryan suddenly remembered.

Stephen, Jake . . . Nina. Lucy Swift. Jeanne Wilder. A thousand other names that he didn't know and probably never would. Names meticulously noted down in Jake's binder of maps and clippings. Names emblazoned on the front pages of newspapers, pictures stuck up on telegraph poles and the doors of the mall.

Slowly, he drew his hand away from Adam's. "I . . . this isn't why I came," he said hesitantly.

"What?" Adam's face contorted in confusion, and the first signs of annoyance. "What the hell does that mean?"

Bryan backed away a few steps, shaking his head. "This isn't why I came, Adam," he said painfully. "It's not what this was about."

"It's not about this?" Adam was shouting now. "It was always about this! What do you mean, it's not what you came here for? You came here for me!"

"Yes. I did," Bryan agreed slowly. "I came here for you." He took another, firmer step away. "And that's where we're going wrong, because you've got me thinking like I came here for me."

Adam followed him, gray eyes dark and blazing. "You're not making sense."

"Maybe not, but I think I'm right." He carried on edging backwards. "I didn't come here to make it better, Adam, I didn't come so we could stick a Band-Aid over the wounds and pretend it never happened. I came here to make it *stop*."

"You can do that," Adam told him earnestly. "You can put it back the way it was."

"I know. But that's no good. It has to be better than the way it was."

The Dark Man's deal was so tempting . . . to have Adam back, to live his life the way it always should have been . . . but that wasn't enough, was it? That didn't bring it to an end. *He* would be okay again, but what about everybody else? All the other families who'd lost people, all the others who were *going* to lose people . . .

He could have Adam back. He could have Adam back, but only if he gave up the battle; only if he turned around and walked away. Only if he left the Dark Man to continue as he'd always done, stealing Redford's children, sucking the life and soul out of the town.

Adam's eyes narrowed. "You don't want me back. That's what you're saying."

"I can't *have* you back," Bryan said, the words hurting as much as he knew they were true. "That's what I'm saying."

"You *can*," Adam insisted urgently. "Bry, aren't you even listening to me?"

"I'm listening," he said slowly. "I'm listening even harder than you think I am." He stopped. "If the Dark Man dies, so do you—that's what you said."

"I'm in his world now, Bryan," Adam reminded him. "Only you can pull me out."

"And I can only do it if I walk away and let him go. That's right, isn't it? That's the price. There's no way to get rid of him without . . ." He faltered slightly. "Without getting rid of you."

Whatever shadow of Adam lingered in this place, whether it was false or real, it was all he had left. If he should somehow truly wipe the Dark Man out, remove his influence from the town forever . . . then Adam would be lost too. He couldn't be free of the Dark Man without giving up everything he had left of his brother.

"Let him *go*?" Adam echoed in disbelief. "Bryan, what the hell d'you think you're doing? You think you can *fight* him?"

"I think I *am* fighting him," Bryan said quietly. "Thirteen steps, Adam."

Thirteen steps to the Dark Man's door, won't be turning back no more. The line that had echoed through his mind a thousand times, a million, suddenly sounded different. That was what he'd been doing all this time; turning back, retreating into the past. Living the same sunny afternoon, again and again and again. Locked in a circle.

Just as those kids who'd been murdered all those years ago had been locked in *their* last moments, reliving the nightmare even beyond death. They'd pulled the whole town with them into the terror of living under the shadow of the Dark Man. Because they couldn't let go.

Sooner or later, somebody had to let go.

He looked across at Adam. "The Dark Man makes everybody face their greatest fears—well, I know what mine is. I'm afraid of admitting it's over. It's over, Adam. It's over, you're dead, and it's *too late*. It doesn't matter how many times I drag myself back here, I'm not gonna be able to save you. And it's time to stop trying."

"You're giving up?" said Adam harshly.

"I'm moving on." Bryan looked at his brother, and smiled sadly. "I'm sorry, Adam. I'm sorrier than you'll ever know. But I didn't kill you, and it's not my fault, and I can't bring you back. I'm sorry."

He turned away. And took the final step.

There was a rushing sensation in his ears and in his head, as if he were falling from a great height. Flashes of images assailed him, too fast to be sure if they were real or only his mind painting random shapes. Memories of Adam, moments with Stephen and Jake, nightmares of the Dark Man . . .

Suddenly it was dark. He couldn't tell if he was in a huge open space or trapped in a tiny enclosure; the air itself felt heavy, pressing tightly down on him as if he were buried in sand. None of his senses could tell him anything . . . and yet somehow, he knew he wasn't alone. He could sense them out there, a crowd huddled around him like fascinated children.

Because they *were* children. Children who'd never grown up, but had stayed behind, trapped in their own pain. Trapping everybody else in their own pain.

"Listen to me," Bryan said hoarsely. His own voice sounded odd to him, and he wasn't entirely sure he was truly speaking aloud. "You have to . . . This has to stop. It's done, okay?" His voice cracked slightly as he thought of Adam. "I came here, and I walked along the steps, and . . . I did it. I made it here to find the secret. But that's not . . . That's not enough. The Dark Man is here because *you're* holding him here. Like I'm holding Adam here. And it's never gonna end unless you let go."

His words fell into endless silence, swallowed up. He had no way of telling if anyone or anything was listening.

"Something terrible happened, and it kept you here," he continued. "Like it's keeping *me* here. It's been five years and I haven't gone anywhere. Just . . . living the same thing over and over again, because if you keep going back then it's not over, it's not forgotten. But you *can't* keep living it over and over. You can't just stay in the same place forever. Sooner or later *somebody* has to move on." Still silence.

"I don't want to leave Adam behind," he said raggedly, "I don't *want* to. But I can't . . ." He bit his lip. "There's nothing else I can do. I can't keep coming back. This isn't the way it's supposed to be. And I don't know what happens when you die, and I don't know where you go or if you're supposed to go anywhere. But you're not supposed to be here. As long as you hold on to it, it's just gonna keep *happening,* and nobody can get out. I can't live and you can't die, and nobody's going anywhere."

He fell silent, breathing heavily. "Sooner or later, you've got to get back up on the trail and go somewhere," he said softly.

Bryan stepped forward, feeling as if he were trying to shoulder his way through something almost solid. Abruptly, the pressure ceased, and he fell forward into bright sunshine.

Hands caught him by the elbows. As Stephen and Jake

helped him up, he suddenly felt compelled to suck in air, as if he'd been living on low oxygen without even knowing it.

"What happened?" Jake asked urgently. Bryan blinked at him, still off balance. His eyes were blurry with afterimages, and it took a moment to be able to see clearly in the afternoon sunshine.

"What did you see?" Bryan asked.

"Nothing!" Jake's eyes narrowed. "You just . . . walked across the stones. Going really slowly, and wobbling like crazy—I thought you were going to fall off."

"I nearly did," he admitted quietly.

Bryan lurched and nearly fell flat on his face as Stephen abruptly let go of his arm, rushing over to his sister. "Nina! You okay?" he asked urgently. The younger girl was stirring as if gradually pulling herself out of a dream.

For a second Nina's eyes were unfocused, and then they cleared. "Stephen? What are you doing here?" she frowned.

Stephen's concern instantly became a disinterested shrug, as he let go of his sister's arm and straightened his jacket. "Nothing," he insisted quickly. "I'm just here with Bryan and Jake."

"Did Mum send you after me?" she asked suspiciously.

"Oh, like she would."

Nina pouted. "You guys are always checking up on me. I'm not *six*, you know. I can go down to . . . the woods . . . if I want to . . ." Her tone wavered in the middle of the irritable declaration as she took in her surroundings, and probably couldn't quite remember how she'd come there or why.

She swung around aimlessly, and lit up as she saw the trail of stones. "Hey, look! I *told* you there was stuff in these woods. It's the Devil's Footsteps stones, just like the rhyme."

179

She moved towards them, and Stephen made a panicked lunge to stop her. Bryan stopped him with an arm across his chest, looking past him into the shadows at the far end of the clearing. Just on the edge of his vision, like afterimages lingering, he could swear he saw faint figures standing watching. "It's okay, Stephen," he said quietly. Stephen shot him a nervously skeptical look, but allowed himself to be pulled back.

Fighting off the Dark Man couldn't work, any more than waking from a single nightmare could save you from bad dreams. You had to go deeper, down to the source. Down to the *reason*.

The Dark Man had grown up around a terrible secret, long buried. But he and the others had dug for the truth, fought their way down to the heart of it and not given up. And now . . . Now it was down to the tortured spirits who lingered in this place.

They'd lain restlessly buried here for decades, anchoring the darkness to a town that had forgotten they'd even existed. After so long, could they let go of that? Would they? The Dark Man was the only shadow of their existence that remained, and they clung tightly to it—just as Bryan had clung to the torture of reliving what had happened to Adam, because that was better than admitting he was gone.

They watched Nina approach the stones. Ignoring the drama behind her, she skipped up to the Footsteps, and made her way along as easily as if they were nothing more than a chalked hopscotch grid. "One in fire, two in blood, three in storm and four in flood," she half sang. Bryan fancied he could hear faint, ghostly whispers echoing the words along with her.

"Five in anger, six in hate, seven fear and evil eight."

Stephen and Jake exchanged tense glances, and Bryan reached out to grip each of them by the wrist. He mouthed the words along with Nina and the half-heard ghost-voices. "Nine in sorrow, ten in pain. Eleven death, twelve life again."

As they came to the final part, Bryan smiled faintly, and spoke the words aloud. "Thirteen steps to the Dark Man's door—won't be turning back no more." This was it; it was done, it was over. He could feel it.

Nina hopped from the final stone and turned around triumphantly to place her hands on her hips. Then she yelped and scrambled backwards as the earth began to shake.

"What the hell—?" Jake began. Stephen started to run towards his sister, and Bryan hastily yanked him back from the stones. There was a loud *crack*, and suddenly the Devil's Footsteps were sinking into the ground, disappearing from view.

"Whoa," said Stephen, eyes wide. They all stood frozen as the rumbles subsided.

Bryan was the first to move forward. He kneeled beside the newly opened fissure in the earth, and looked down.

It was full of bones. Children's bones.

~ Epilogue ~

STANDING THERE IN THE WOODS with the police everywhere felt . . . strange. Like coming full circle. Only now it wasn't Adam's disappearance they were investigating, but his finding.

A frighteningly large number of small skeletons had been hauled out of the hole, with more still coming even now. One of them was probably Adam's; he decided it was easier not knowing which. Perhaps testing might eventually reveal the identities of them all . . . and perhaps somebody, somewhere, might be able to find the names of the children who had first been secretly buried here, and put them to rest at last.

Just as all the other children who'd disappeared in the decades since could finally be laid to rest.

The unnerved-looking detectives who had questioned him and the others were already muttering about cults and serial killers. Perhaps Redford's disease of the memory still lingered to some extent, or perhaps they would just rather not confront any more difficult truth. Bryan didn't suppose it mattered; whatever power the Dark Man had held here in the woods was long gone.

So were the other witnesses to its destruction.

Stephen had hauled his little sister back home, Nina protesting all the way because she wanted to stay and see them dig out the skeletons. Jake had been forced to leave not long after, apologetically pleading that his parents had been waiting long enough. And then Bryan was alone, watching the police at their work. Probably they should have chased him away, but nobody did. It was starting to rain.

"Bryan!"

He jumped at his name, almost unfamiliar although he knew the voice that had uttered it. He turned to see his father running towards him, slipping and sliding on the slick mud. It was strange to be grabbed by the shoulders, examined, as if he was *there*, as if he mattered.

"Bryan, are you all right?"

"I, uh, yeah, um . . . yeah." He stumbled on the question, not expecting it, not sure how to take it.

Just as he didn't know how to take it when his father tugged him closer with an arm around his shoulder, turned to look at the police excavation. Bryan looked up to see his father's face creased with fear and worry; dark emotions, but real ones, honest ones, instead of the horrible blank numbness.

"Your mother's bringing round the car. She'll be here any second."

And Bryan choked on that, too—the idea of his mother not just out of bed on a Sunday but in the car, driving it, moving with a set destination in mind instead of just drifting.

It wasn't any easier for Bryan to believe when she came dashing out of the trees to join them than when his father had. "Bryan?" She sounded scared, shocked, worried, as if she'd woken up in the middle of a nightmare.

And Bryan loved it.

He gestured vaguely towards the policemen, still not totally sure this was even happening. "They . . . er, we, er . . . I found the stones. Thirteen stones in the middle of the woods."

"Just like you said," his father said quietly.

"So many bones . . . ," breathed his mother, face pinched by distress.

His father closed his eyes. "But at least . . . they can be laid to rest now. And even if, even if . . ." He trailed off, and tightened his grip on Bryan's shoulder. "Well, it's better than not knowing."

"Yeah. Yeah, it is," agreed Bryan.

They stood together, in the rain, watching the policemen work. And it didn't feel like the end of everything, so much as a pause for breath before a new direction.

About the Author

E. E. Richardson wrote *Devil's Footsteps* while at university in England, studying for a degree in cybernetics.